THIRTY DAYS OF HATE

GINGER TALBOT

Thirty Days of Hate

Copyright 2018 by Ginger Talbot

Thanks so much for buying "Thirty Days of Hate"! If you'd like to be notified of future releases, freebies, contests and more, please sign up for my newsletter at https://app.getresponse.com/site2/gingertalbot?u=B1VF6&webforms_id=AI0D

CHAPTER ONE

March, Pevlova Oblast, several hours east of St. Petersburg

WILLOW

How could I have given my heart to a perfect liar?

That's the question I'm asking myself as my lungs burn, as my legs slash through the dark night, as my boots slide across grimy snow. I came here to find out the truth of Sergei, and I think that very soon, it's going to kill me.

Sergei, the man I love and loathe in equal measure, may or may not be the person behind the series of kidnappings of young girls from local nightclubs. Girls like the blonde I'm hauling along with me right now, in a desperate race to reach the police station.

When the girls disappear, they're never seen again, but there are dark whispers. Trafficking. Whorehouses. Rape and torture.

Some of the rumors say that Sergei is the man behind the kidnappings. Some say it's *Cataha*.

Some even say that they're one and the same. Or working together.

Or bitter rivals in the same trade.

The lies fall from everyone's lips in hushed whispers, and I am further from learning the truth than I was when I arrived in Russia five months ago.

But I refuse to be an idle observer to the horror that continues to unfold here. I've been working with a local group of volunteers, to intercept the kidnappers and expose whoever is behind it all.

Whoever. Even if that means the man I was foolish enough to fall for. If it turns out that it's Sergei, I'll kill him at the first opportunity. Never mind that it will be the same as killing myself.

We volunteers dress up in our fake designer clothes like all the other club-goers. We wear our disguises, wigs, hair extensions, sunglasses, colored contact lenses, different makeup, the men wearing different types of facial hair. Never looking the same twice.

Last week I was a redhead. This week I'm a brunette, with long, flowing hair extensions.

When we go to the clubs, we dance and pretend to drink, but all the while we're scanning the crowds, looking out for men who are slipping drugs into women's drinks.

We secretly take pictures of the men with our cell phones, then move forward to warn the women of what's happening. We've saved fourteen girls so far, and reported three "scouts", as they call them, to the police. The scouts have been arrested.

I've been lucky so far, but nobody's lucky forever. Not when they take as many stupid chances as I do.

Going to the American-themed Club Hollywood tonight was especially risky, because we've been tipped off that the owner is working with the traffickers.

But knowing that, we couldn't sit idle.

Just a little while ago, I followed one of the bouncers and his intended victim out of the club. A beautiful girl with thick blonde hair hanging halfway down her back, wearing a cheap, stained white parka and grimy white boots. She didn't know it, but she was advertising herself as perfect bait. Pretty, from a poor family, who wouldn't be missed if she was taken. The bouncer flirted with her, bought her a drink, and then waited a few minutes until the drug kicked in.

As the man steered her past the bouncers outside, she was staggering, the effects of the drug already pumping through her system. Fortunately, she'd only had a couple of sips, despite his urging, or she'd have been in even worse shape.

I pretended to be drunk, stumbling along behind them.

Club Hollywood is in an industrial district, right on the border of a run-down block of apartment buildings. At night, the lights from the front of the club bathe the entire block in sickly yellow, but the parking lot, a block to the right of the club, is only lit up at the front. The back of the lot is a yawning black hole.

I made my move as soon as he maneuvered her out of the light, towards the back of the lot. I ran up behind him, my boots crunching noisily on the crusty layer of ice over the snow. He started to turn towards me, letting go of the blonde woman's arm. Gasping for breath in the chill night air, I jabbed him in the neck with a needle. I'd practiced that move for months, in the apartments of various friends I was crashing with, using an empty syringe and a dummy.

He staggered, his broad, flat face twisting with rage. He struggled to stay upright, feet suddenly gone stupid. Not listening to instructions from his brain.

"See how it feels, you bastard?" I shouted at him. The

girls he'd drugged, the horror that they'd felt when they'd realized what was happening to them... The raw terror, the helplessness, the betrayal of one's own body... He was feeling all of it.

Slowly, he crumpled and fell onto his left side, with a satisfyingly hard crash on the icy pavement. His jaw was working, his tongue suddenly too thick to form words.

The blonde stumbled back a step and gaped at me, her eyes unfocused.

She tried to speak, but her words came out in a mumbled slurry of saliva. "Whash happen..."

I couldn't imagine what would have happened if she'd finished her drink. She'd have been down on the ground unconscious, I imagined.

"You've been drugged," I told her quickly. "That asshole drugged your drink – he was going to kidnap you." I grabbed her arm to steady her. "We're going back to the nightclub now, in case any of his friends are waiting out here. We're going to call an ambulance once we're inside the club."

Triumph flared inside me, a source of warmth on this cold, evil night. This would be enough for Akim to publish an article in *Reforma*, naming this nightclub and forcing an investigation. This would be the third nightclub our group had shut down in as many months.

Everything felt so good at that moment. Everything was working the way it should, for once. The gears of justice clicking into place and turning, grinding evil to a pulp between their cold metal teeth.

And then everything flew to pieces.

Three men came pounding down the sidewalk, bearing down on us. They were a solid wall of muscular fury between us and our escape route. Where had they come from? They were like demons bursting out of hell, material-izing out of thin air.

Seconds later, my two lookouts, Simon and Yakov, shot out of an alley across the street, yelling, waving their arms, cans of mace in their hands. The three men turned and fired at them with silenced weapons. Simon and Yakov folded like rag dolls in the middle of the street.

And now my friends are dead and the police station might as well be a million miles away, because we'll never reach it in time.

I'm dead. The blonde is dead. Oh, we're still breathing for now, but we don't have a chance in frozen hell of surviving the night.

The police station is ten blocks away in the opposite direction. The second I saw my friends fall, I turned and ran across the street, dragging her with me.

We won't make it, but we'll die trying.

My heart is shattering into pieces for my two dead friends, but I can't spare any breath for crying. I need it for running. And very soon, probably, screaming.

She's staggering and slowing me down. I should drop her in the snow to save myself, but instead, I grip her arm tighter.

"Move your ass!" I shriek at her.

"Leave me," the blonde slurs, her head lolling. "Shhhlow you down. Can't feel maaa legssshhh..."

"No!"

I start screaming at the top of my lungs for help.

We're passing an apartment building now, one of those ugly old Soviet-era blocks of concrete. Not a single door or window opens. If anything, I can almost feel the buildings hugging themselves shut, the people inside cowering with their hands clapped over their ears.

Here, in the land where poverty chews up lives and every traffic stop is the choice of a bribe or prison, good Samaritans are few and far between.

And they don't live very long.

The men are gaining on us, and the true horror of what's about to happen engulfs me, and I want to weep.

I always knew it would end this way. I've done a little good. I've saved a few girls. A pitifully small number. I just hoped I'd have more time.

Then the blonde pulls away from me, deliberately, and throws herself on the ground. Now I have a terrible choice. And it's a choice that I must make in microseconds.

She's sacrificing herself.

If I stay with her, I'm committing suicide. If I run, there is the chance, the faintest of chances, that I'll be able to get help for her.

"I'll come for you!" I scream into the wind, but I'm talking more to myself than to her. I run as fast as I can, my tears freezing to my cheeks. The muscles in my legs are on fire, and every panicked, icy breath burns my lungs.

Keep moving, keep moving, keep moving...

But her sacrifice is in vain. I only make it about another block before someone pops out from between two parked cars and a hood is thrown over my head. They move so fast that I barely have time to react before my world is swallowed in darkness.

I pretend to go limp, and someone picks me up from behind. I've lost, I know this, but I will fight every step of the way.

Fear pumping through my veins like acid, I lift my legs, hook them behind his knees, and send him crashing to the ground. He lands on top of me, a thousand-ton pile of bricks dropped right on my ribcage.

The snow barely breaks our fall. The breath is knocked out of me, stars explode behind my eyes, and I taste blood in my mouth. I gag on the reek of vodka fumes, B.O. and cigarette smoke. His massive weight is crushing me, and he's cursing at me as he rolls off.

I'm temporarily stunned, my muscles jellied and my head whirling, as I'm scooped up and tossed into the back of a vehicle like a sack of flour. The ice-rink-cold of the floor shocks me back awake.

The metallic clang of a door slamming rings in my ears, and we start moving.

I'm lying curled on my side, and my hands are free. Why didn't he secure my hands? Probably because he knows that he and his men don't have a damn thing to fear from me. I am torn between the fear of seeing what's waiting for me, and the fear of not seeing it.

I yank the hood off and sit up.

I'm in the back of a truck. There are no windows; it's a metal prison without hope of escape.

There are four men in the back of the truck, sitting on benches. All armed. But it's the one wearing a devil's mask with curling horns who sets my heart racing in panic. He's got a scar on his neck, which means it's really him, not a copycat.

Cataha. The scar comes from a recent assassination attempt by a rival gang. One of the rumors I heard was that Sergei and his men were behind the attempt. But another story being whispered among frightened denizens of the underworld is that Sergei is *Cataha*, and he was injured when the police came for him.

The mask is something new, from what I've heard, something he only started wearing a few months ago.

He's leaning back against the wall, his rifle resting on his broad thighs, and I think he's looking at me, but it's hard to tell in the dim light, with the dark eyeholes of the mask obscuring his gaze.

I shudder and look away, staring at the floor. I finally have the answer to one of the many questions that's been tormenting me ever since that horrible night in California eight months ago, when Sergei broke my heart.

Sergei is not *Cataha*.

CHAPTER TWO

I know Sergei intimately. I know the shape of him, every curve of his muscles, the broad spread of his chest, even the way he breathes. I can feel him before he walks into a room, an intimate connection that envelops me and pulls me to him with irresistible force.

The bastard in the mask is tall, broad and burly, but he's not my Sergei.

My Sergei. That's a bitterly unfunny joke. He was never mine.

I rub my head, still aching from being slammed on the sidewalk, and squint in the dim light.

The blonde is there, and she's curled up in a ball, head lolling, sucking in gulping breaths.

There are two dark forms sprawled on the floor. Simon and Yakov. Their chests are rising and falling, and I don't see or smell any blood. I realize that they must have been shot with tranquilizer darts. That's why I didn't hear any gunshots. The traffickers wanted them alive.

And it wasn't out of mercy.

They're keeping us alive to interrogate us, to find out

everything they can about our anti-trafficking efforts. They'll demand the names of all our friends. Our plans. Our methods. They'll slash and stab and burn the flesh right off us, leave us weeping and pleading for death through shattered teeth.

Then Yakov and Simon will be murdered very slowly, and their bodies dumped in a public place, to set an example for the rest of the anti-trafficking community. As for the blonde girl and me, if we survive the interrogation with our looks reasonably intact, we'll be raped by our captors, then sold to be raped by wealthy perverts for the rest of our shortened lives.

In a couple of hours, when we fail to check in with Akim, she'll figure out that we were kidnapped and she'll alert the police, but it will be too late.

We always tell her about our missions before we go out – in case we fail to return. Yes, *her*. Akim is a woman – named Ludmilla. The woman Sergei claimed to be married to. But Ludmilla isn't married. I have no idea what Sergei's lie means, and now I'll probably never find out.

We'll be martyrs. Akim will write our story, the tale of a brave team of vigilantes snatched up by traffickers. It's a new twist on an age-old tale. The story of our disappearance will capture international attention. Once again the ugly reality of the modern-day slave trade will briefly singe the consciences of those sitting at home safe in their living rooms.

But it's cold comfort, especially because I failed to save the girl.

Our only way out is suicide. We are always prepared for capture. We take cyanide pills on every rescue mission, and other hidden tools. I've got little blades and a handcuff key concealed in the hair extensions that I wore for this mission.

Simon and Yakov wear leather bracelets with blades tucked inside.

Cataha hands his rifle to one of the other men, reaches into a black gym bag that's lying at his feet, and pulls out a handful of syringes. My stomach curdles, and I huddle in on myself. There's nowhere to run, and no fight left in me. As we bounce along the road, he kneels down and jabs Simon and then Yakov in the leg, through their pants.

Then he moves towards the blonde, who tries to crawl away from him, and he jabs her in the ass. She cries out in pain, scrabbling at the floor with her hands.

"Antidote," he sneers. "It'll wake you up, so you can enjoy what's coming next." I think his accent places him from Moscow. Something about his voice bothers me, but I can't think what.

Now Simon and Yakov are sitting up and groaning in pain. Skinny young men, eyes huge with fright. They both volunteered because girls in their family have disappeared – Simon's cousin, Yakov's sister.

They'll die for their bravery.

We ride in silence, the truck bouncing over the rutted road.

Huddled up in a ball, I sneak glances at *Cataha* through the curtain of my long, fake locks. He doesn't say a word to us. Is he watching us? I can't tell.

Much too soon, the truck comes to a stop and the back door clangs open, and one of the men growls, "Get out!" So we obey, stumbling out into the dirty snow.

I do a quick visual sweep of the area, trying to orient myself. We're parked in front of a building with taped-up, cracked windows, and a sign identifying it as a tire shop. The chain link fence around the front yard sags, torn in places, and brown weeds poke up through the snow. The other buildings around us are even more decrepit. The only illumination is from the headlights of the truck we were in and three other trucks pulling up. There are no street lights, no lights in the windows, no sign of life. Nobody to hear us scream.

There's a generator hooked up to the building; the loud clanking thrum of its motor beats against my eardrums. So, an abandoned building without power.

The men are crowding around us. At least ten of them, because they've been joined by the men from the other three trucks. We're marched inside, guns jabbing us in our ribcages to keep us moving. We exchange despairing glances; I hate the fear and hopelessness in Simon and Yakov's eyes, because I know it mirrors my own.

The heat's on, low, just enough to take the chill off the air. Then we're moved down the hallway into a dark room with one lone fluorescent light flickering overhead, and forced to shed our coats at gunpoint.

The men pat us down, running their hands everywhere. Hands sliding between my legs, over my breasts, as I grit my teeth and restrain myself from crying out or flinching. I won't give them the satisfaction.

They think they're being thorough, and they search all the obvious places, but they miss a lot. My cyanide pill stays hidden in my hollow bracelet, my blades and handcuff key are still in my hair.

They're stupid. They're amateurs. That's a good thing, right?

But there are so many of them, and we have no weapons.

Then one of the men barks "Sit!" and points at a row of folding chairs that face a blank wall. The blonde woman sits at the end of the row, I sit next to her, then Yakov, and Simon.

I glance at Yakov, and I see tears glittering in his eyes. He's engaged to be married. She's expecting.

He manages a woeful smile. "It's all right," he whispers miserably, but it isn't, and we both know it.

As we settle in, I scan the room. Oil-stained concrete floor. A space-heater humming in the corner. A bunch of equipment that I don't recognize at the back of the room.

Every second thunders by, jabbing at me. Our time is running out.

I'm in as little pain as I'm ever going to be in, from now until the end of my life.

That thought makes me furious. And it snaps me back to reality. I have to stop wallowing in hopelessness. I can't focus on what might or might not happen to me in the future; I have no control over it. All I can do is look for opportunities. To escape, or to die quickly.

The blonde mutters something, and I lean in to hear what she said.

"That isn't the real *Cataha*."

"How do you know?" I whisper.

"Because I met him, before he started wearing his mask. This guy has a different body shape. And he smells different."

I look at her in astonishment. "You met him and lived?"

"Barely." Her voice is a bleak wasteland of despair. Because she was incredibly lucky to survive an encounter with him, and now her luck has run out.

I reach out and take her hand. "What's your name?" I murmur.

"Darya."

I roll the cyanide pill into her palm. "I'm Natasha," I say, giving her the name on my fake papers. "Cyanide. Wait until the last second," I whisper to her. "When you're sure there's no hope. You don't have to use it if you don't want to."

She nods dully. "I'll want to. You kept one for yourself?"

"Yes."

I'm lying. But I am the one who failed to save this girl. I gave her hope, I promised her we'd be all right, and we still ended up here in the middle of a nightmare. I can't free her, I can't give her a future, a husband, children, freedom from terror. The only gift I can give her is to die on her own terms. It's a horrible gift, a heartbreaking gift, but it's better than letting the traffickers determine her fate.

I've got my little blades and a good working knowledge of human anatomy, and I hope I can puncture an artery and bleed out before the men start in on me.

I hear them moving around the back of the room, behind us. Why are they drawing this out?

I'm sick of feeling helpless.

I look at the fake *Cataha* and stretch my lips into a broad, deliberate smile. Nothing pisses off men like him more than seeing women who aren't afraid. I should know; I was raised by exactly this kind of man.

He walks over and raps my head with the barrel of his gun. Not too hard; he must be saving the real pain for later.

"You think this is funny, bitch?" he snaps at me.

"We've got a friend who's going to report us missing to the police. She'll already have called."

"Which police department? The Pevlovagrad police?" he sneers. He turns to the doorway behind us and calls, "Send him in!"

I twist around to see...and the Pevlovagrad police chief, Jakob Ivanov, walks through the doorway. The shock hits me like a tidal wave of ice-cold water. Rage at his betrayal chokes me.

Akim has always told us he is one of the good ones.

I glare at him in disgust, then return my attention to the fake *Cataha*. "There's more than one police chief. More than one department."

"And this is the woman you think will call the police for you?" He yells out again. "Send her in."

I can't keep the dismay and fear from my face.

No.

But yes.

Akim-Ludmilla walks through the door, her slate-gray eyes as cold as ice as she flicks me an indifferent glance, and my throat closes in horror. A pretty woman of about thirty years old, she has dark auburn hair, high cheekbones, and lines on her forehead. Her hair has a streak of gray. I've been told that happened after her sister was abducted years ago.

Yakov and Simon jerk in shock when they recognize her, their chairs squeaking. They flash me panicked looks.

Why would she do this to us? *Why?* Was Ludmilla bribed? Threatened?

She looks calm and unruffled.

I cannot believe this.

I had utter and complete faith in her. That's why I sought her out when we started going on our rescue missions. She knows the contact information of most of our volunteers; she's done anonymous interviews with them that were featured in *Reforma*. And now they'll be hunted down and killed.

"Enjoy the show," the fake *Cataha* barks. Suddenly I realize what's bothering me about his voice – it's completely normal. I'd heard that *Cataha's* voice was raspy from the attack.

Darya's right, he is a fake.

Then the movie starts playing, projected on the wall in front of us, and I go stiff with rage and disgust. The video shows a nude woman with a noose around her neck, in a brightly lit white room that's devoid of furniture or decoration. Her hands are tied behind her back. There's a beam running across the ceiling, and the rope is strung over it. *Cataha* is standing next to her, holding the end of the rope.

Darya stiffens with fear and looks at the screen. "I think that's the real one," she whispers to me.

On the screen, *Cataha* starts pulling the rope, grunting with effort, and horror floods through me.

The naked woman is lifted off the ground, and her legs kick frantically, then she's lowered again seconds later. *Cataha* loosens the noose with his fingers.

She gasps and wheezes and makes inarticulate noises, her eyes enormous pools of despair. *Cataha* pulls the end of the rope again, and she's hauled back into the air. Her legs thrash, and *Cataha* throws his head back and barks out a hideous laugh.

Yakov is sobbing, his shoulders shaking. Simon vomits on the floor. Tears stream down Darya's face, but she doesn't make a sound.

This is what they do to people who cross them.

I try to look away, and one of the men raps the gun against my head and snarls, "Watch!"

The hell with this. I've been taking self-defense classes continuously for almost a year now, and while I'm no match for these men in hand-to-hand combat, I have one thing to my advantage: the element of surprise. Nobody looks at skinny, nondescript me and thinks I have any fight in me. So while they're busy underestimating me, I'm good for a quick, disabling strike, although after that I'm a dead girl walking.

I spring to my feet and kick him in the crotch before he has time to react, and yank the gun out of his hand. I will go down shooting. We all will.

I aim the gun at his throat and squeeze the trigger – and am shocked to see that it's firing darts, not bullets.

Do *all* their guns have tranquilizer darts instead of bullets? Why? The only thing my panicked brain can come up with is that they are determined to keep us alive for the interrogation. It still feels off, but I don't have time to ponder that right now.

The room explodes into chaos. Darya falls to the ground and crawls away on her hands and knees. Simon launches himself at one of our captors, and they crash to the ground in a tangle of limbs. I shoot Ludmilla in the chest, the dart quivering right above her left breast. The other men are shouting, rushing towards me.

I feel a strange crackling in the air, a nervous anticipation. There's only one person who makes me feel that way.

Then the door flies open, and a man barrels through and bellows, "Enough!" And my heart stops in my chest.

Because the man is Sergei.

CHAPTER THREE

I feel bloodless, weightless, as I stare at him. More men are pouring past him. The gun drops from my fingers and I hear it clatter on the concrete.

Sergei. I haven't seen him in so long. Eight long months. I almost stopped believing he was real. He was an idea, a concept, a dream and a nightmare.

Now he's flesh again.

He looms big in the doorway. He's wearing a black leather coat lined with shearling, and the air around him crackles with rage and power. That face – those cruel, sensual lips, those broad Slavic cheekbones, the scar slashing through his eyebrow...oh, how I've missed that beautiful face.

I thought I'd never see him again. I even did my best to make sure of it. I had the GPS tracker that he'd implanted on me removed after he left me. I was trying to find him here, sure, but only so I could find out if he really was married and a pimp, not so I could see him in person.

What would be the point, after he crumpled me up like trash and threw me away?

As he storms towards me, my body responds to him the same way it always does, singing with lust, betraying me. I accept that, and I violently shove it aside. After what Sergei did to me, I grew stronger. I can separate my mind from the needs of my body.

And I will never love a trafficker.

Crave him, yes. Love him? No.

Darya scrambles to her feet, looking from him to me and back, in confusion.

"You motherfucker," I spit at him. "You sick bastard! Come to gloat?"

"You know him?" Darya stares at me in shock.

I swallow a bitter taste. "I knew him. No, scratch that – I never knew him at all. Let's just say he and I have met."

She nods, looking sad and sympathetic. "Ah, I see. You fell for him and he betrayed you into trafficking."

She thinks she understands, but she's not even close.

She has no idea how complicated this is. How sick, evil and heart-breaking.

How beautifully and perfectly Sergei played me, without ever appearing to. How he tortured and teased my body until I couldn't tell where pain ended and pleasure began.

How he mocked me when I told him that I loved him. The only man I've ever said those words to. And now those words will never leave my lips again.

"What the hell do you think you're playing at?" Sergei roars at me, towering over me, and the air crackles with electricity and rage.

"Playing at?" I choke out the words, and I am horrified to realize I'm sobbing. I can't help myself; tears pour down my cheeks. I held back the tears when I thought that Simon and Yakov were dead, but now my body is shaking with sobs. What's wrong with me? Why am I such a horrible person? "I'm not playing at a damn thing! Just because everything is a game to *you* – you're not even human!" I leap to my feet and launch myself at him with a strangled cry, and two of his men lunge forward and haul me away.

The room is filling up with his men, a small army of them, and they hustle us back out onto the street. We don't have our coats anymore, it's the middle of the night, and it's freezing. We are separated from Simon and Yakov. I can hear them shouting as they're forced into the back of a truck, and I feel sick with rage and fear.

We all told ourselves that we were prepared for something like this, but how can you be? Prepared for the threat of torture, of rape, of an agonizing death? Prepared for seeing your friends flayed alive or eviscerated?

I can't see Sergei anymore. He's left me again. That's what he does best, isn't it? I hate him so much right now.

I want him so much right now.

I want to travel back in time to when he lay in my bed with me and held me in his strong arms and made me feel safe and loved. That love was a lie, but it was such a beautiful lie that I wanted to wrap it around me and live inside it forever. Oh, how I've missed his body, his fierce strength, his feather-soft kisses. The smell of him, musky and masculine. His muscles bunching as he gathered me close and pressed me up against him. How I've missed thinking that I was so special to him, that I'd penetrated that thick armor around his heart when nobody else could.

How I've missed the rage that radiated from him when anyone threatened to hurt me.

But now he's the one doing the hurting.

I'm jerked back to the present, shivering violently in the bitterly cold night as Darya and I are handcuffed.

I imagine myself with superhuman strength, lifting Sergei over my head and hurling him into a live volcano. Watching him sink into the molten lava.

The image only makes me sad and panicked. I ask myself for the millionth time – what the hell is wrong with me? Why am I like this?

One of the men opens the back of a truck and gestures at it. We climb in awkwardly, with the men boosting us, our knees banging on the floor.

The door clangs shut and the truck starts driving. At least there's some heat back here. And most importantly, we're alone.

I finally feel a spark of optimism.

Ha. Handcuffs? Locked door?

I've only practiced for this for close to a year now, from every possible position.

We're rattling over potholed streets again, the truck bouncing and jerking.

"Darya, I have a handcuff key hidden in my hair extensions." My voice bounces off the walls, in our cold, vile echo chamber. "I'm going to lie down on the floor so you can reach it," I say. If I had to, I could kick my boots off and get the key myself with my toes, but it will be faster if she helps me. As I lie there with my cheek pressed against cold metal, she fumbles around, and I direct her until she finds it. She drops it into my open hands.

"Stay there," I instruct her. I maneuver the key into the tiny hole on her handcuffs, and I breathe a sigh of relief when I hear the click.

She sheds the cuffs as if they're a venomous snake wrapped around her wrists, and then frees me.

I crawl over to the door, pull a lock pick out of my hair extensions, and begin working on it.

"Nice trick. I'll have to remember that," Darya says.

"I've almost got it..." I look at her. We're not dressed for the weather. I'm wearing a sweater and wool pants and boots, and she's wearing a sweater and jeans with leg-warmers, but it's damn cold outside. "We have no coats. I don't know where we are. We may freeze to death out there."

"Better than the alternative." She says it without hesitation. She's brave, she's smart...she deserves so much better than what life has handed her.

I won't let her down a second time.

I go back to working on the lock, trying to manipulate the pick with fingers that are stiff with cold.

Darya speaks. "He was your lover?"

"Something like that. I couldn't really explain what he was."

"If he catches us, will he kill us? Or sell us?"

I wish I could offer her reassurances. I shake my head bleakly. "I have no idea what he'd do. It's safer to assume the worst. I thought I knew him, and I could not have been more wrong. I can't understand him any better than I could understand an alien."

I've got the door lock open. I can hear traffic around us, which means the truck is driving towards the city. Then the truck slows down.

Now is the time.

I kick the door open, and we jump out into the slushy snow. We land hard. Darya grunts in pain, and I stifle a whimper. My whole body hurts.

We're in luck. The truck drives away; apparently the driver has not noticed our escape. I breathe a silent thanks to whoever is watching over us tonight. Thank God we were kidnapped by idiots. Thank you, God, thank you, thank you.

"You did it," Darya gasps. "We're free. We did it. I thought we were going to *die*."

The wind whips my hair into my face. It's well past midnight, I know. We're in a downtown area, but I don't see any signs of life.

"Me too. We've got to get moving before we freeze solid."

We run past apartment buildings and closed shops with metal gates over their windows. Finally, thank heavens, we come to an open tea shop.

We run inside, our teeth chattering like clacking castanets. The warm air is a breath from heaven. My ears start burning as they start to thaw. There are a dozen or so people in there, and they glance at us and then go right back to their tea and conversation. Darya and I, gasping for breath, running through the door without coats in the middle of the night...we look like trouble.

We head over to the counter to order. A short, heavy-set woman in a shapeless brown sweater and a dun-colored skirt that reaches her ankles bustles over. And then it hits me.

"Crud," I groan, patting my pants pockets. "They took my wallet. I have no money. Do you?"

Despair washes over her face. "No, they took my wallet too."

I bite my lip. "We don't have our cell phones. I don't know what to do."

The woman behind the counter shakes her head sympathetically. "If you girls want some nice hot tea, it's on me. Let me take you into the back room, farther away from the door. You'll be warmer there."

Tears fill my eyes at her kindness. After the horror we've

been through tonight, I'm grateful for the reminder that some human beings are decent.

She ushers us into a small room in the back.

"I'll be right back with the tea, you poor things." And she hurries back into the main room, shutting the door behind her.

The warmth is heaven and hell; my ears, fingers and nose are throbbing as they thaw. Darya and I sit there in silence, flexing our fingers to get the circulation back, our breathing slowly returning to normal.

A few minutes later, she brings us tea and cookies.

She even lets me borrow her cell phone, and I quickly send a coded text message to one of the volunteers. The text tells him that we're all burned, and to warn everybody else.

Everybody who's still alive.

"They still have your friends," Darya points out. "What can we do about that? The police chief is in on it. Who can we even call?"

I like her a lot. She's just escaped from a nightmare, and she's still thinking about other people. I'm thinking the same thing, turning it over in my mind. Who can I call in time to save them?

She frowns in thought. "There was a reporter named Akim. That was his code-name, anyway. He actually interviewed me once, on the phone. Akim writes for *Reforma*. We could call him."

Oh, the irony.

She doesn't know. That's because Ludmilla hides her identity very carefully. Most people believe that "Akim" is a man, and she uses a voice changer to disguise her voice when she interviews people on the phone. When I tracked her down a few months ago and told her about the work that my volunteer group was doing, it took her a long time to trust me.

It never occurred to me not to trust *her*.

I shake my head.

"The woman who came into the room after the police chief? That was Akim. Her real name is Ludmilla, and that bitch sold us out," I tell Darya.

Darya looks skeptical. She shakes her head in protest. "No. Akim is a man."

"I've sat right next to her when she was interviewing people on the phone. She uses a voice changer."

"Are you sure?" she asks. I don't blame her. I know it sounds crazy.

"Yes, I'm sure. And you know what? My friends and I told Ludmilla we'd be going to Club Hollywood tonight," I tell Darya. "And now I know how Sergei and his men knew where to find us. She must have told them."

"Who is Sergei?"

"The big, handsome motherfucking son-of-a-bitch bastard back at the warehouse. The one with the knife scar on his eyebrow."

Her brows pinch together in dismay. She shakes her head. "So it's hopeless for your friends? Are you giving up?"

"Never," I say, stung. "I think if we call the newsroom director at *Reforma*, he'll help us. Ludmilla may be corrupt, but I have to believe that the others there don't know. She must have accepted a huge bribe. There are still some good people there. I'll ask the lady behind the counter if I can borrow her phone one more time."

Darya smiles hopefully. "I'm sure it will work! I'm so glad that I met you. You have to tell me more about this group of yours."

But the relief doesn't last long. Neither does my belief

that there are more good people than bad, even in a desperate, poverty-stricken district like the Pevlova Oblast.

Because now I'm starting to feel dizzy. Too dizzy for it to be just from exhaustion. And the room is spinning and I'm struggling not to vomit.

"The teeaaa..." I slur, trying to move my hands, not sure if I said the words out loud.

The nice, sweet lady behind the counter drugged our tea.

And the room winks out of existence. The world goes dark.

CHAPTER FOUR

Someone is shaking me.

"Natasha, wake up!" A woman's voice chants the words over and over.

Who is Natasha? Who is talking to me? Where am I?

Then unwelcome memory returns. I'm Natasha for now, Darya is talking to me, and I have no idea where I am.

I groan as she helps me sit up. I clutch at the mattress and wait for the room to stop moving. Slowly, my head clears. Mattress. I'm on a bed.

"The door and the windows are locked," she tells me. "It's daytime. I don't know who took us, but I don't think anyone raped us while we slept."

"You're way ahead of me. Give me a minute." I struggle to my feet and look around. Panic pushes aside my dizziness.

Why are we here? If somebody drugged us and brought us to a strange place, it can't have been done with good intentions.

But who was behind it?

Leaning against the wall, I take stock of our surroundings.

We're in a big white room with wooden floors. There are expensive-looking rugs on the floors.

At the far end of the room there's a bookshelf stretching to the ceiling and stocked with books, there's a window looking out onto a field of snow and a high chain link fence, and one king-size bed with a soft fluffy blue comforter and piles of pillows.

There are no paintings. There's a desk that holds a jug of water and two glasses. I'm desperately thirsty; I stumble over and pour myself some. As I gulp the water down, I notice that the cup is plastic, and so is the jug. So we won't be able to smash them and use the shards as weapons.

No mirrors on the walls.

I'd bet that the window is shatter-proof.

Someone dressed us while we were unconscious. We're both wearing thin white cotton T-shirts and white yoga pants. I look around the room.

"No shoes," I say. "No boots. No coats. No closet with any other clothes. The choice of clothing is strategic. If we managed to escape from here, we'd freeze to death in minutes."

"Very good," a tinny male voice says, and I'm so startled I drop my glass. Darya stifles a shriek. We look around frantically, but we can't see where the voice came from. There's an intercom somewhere, and someone is watching and listening to us – and they want us to know it.

I stifle the urge to pat my head to see if the blades and lock pick have been removed from my extensions. The long, fake brown locks are still hanging past my shoulders, so I might be in luck. But if someone is listening to us, they're probably also watching us, so I don't want to give away the location of my weapons.

"Son of a bitch," Darya says, shaking her head slowly. "These motherfuckers have some fancy gear."

"Great." I sit back down on the bed, my knees weak. My stomach is growling with hunger. "I always wanted to be kidnapped by a bunch of fancy men. Nothing worse than a low-class kidnapper."

Then I hear footsteps approaching, and we both tense up. I hear the clicking of a latch, and the door opens. A tall, lean, dour-faced man in a butler's uniform stands there.

Wordlessly, he rolls a tray into the room. There are two plates full of stew on the tray, and a loaf of sliced pumpernickel bread. There's a pot of butter with a butter knife, and bowls of fresh-cut fruit salad.

We eat lunch ravenously, not knowing if it's going to be our last meal.

We spend the next few hours pacing around the room or reclining on the bed and talking in hushed whispers. There's a small bathroom, with soap, toothpaste and toothbrushes, but no razors. We each shower quickly, looking around resentfully for video cameras that we can't see.

While I'm the bathroom, I feel the dark mood descend. The mood that makes me want to bang my head against the ceramic until I see stars, that makes me want to scratch and claw at my flesh until I bleed.

The moods come from nowhere. They come from hell. Or my family, who used to kidnap and pimp out women and little children. Ever since I found out what my father really did for a living, I get these attacks from time to time. Not when I'm in the middle of doing anything; when I'm alone, when I pause to take a breath.

Not now. Not now. I have to keep my mind clear for Darya. Maybe I can do something to save her.

I'm digging my nails into the flesh of my leg to satisfy the wordless voices that shriek at me from the void.

Bitch, bitch, bitch... Bleed, bleed, bleed...

I pull my hands away, splash my face with cold water, and I use every bit of strength in my mind and body to force the darkness back.

Someday I won't be able to keep the screams away, and the darkness will claim me. Until that I day, I keep fighting to right past wrongs.

We spend the next few hours in silence.

I listlessly flip through a book without seeing the words on the page. Darya just lies on the bed, curled up on her side, staring at nothing.

Worry gnaws at my insides. Where are Simon and Yakov? What is happening to them right now? I hate this feeling of helplessness.

When the sun starts to dip under the horizon, we hear a rapping on our door.

It's the butler-jailer, gesturing at us to follow him.

Darya and I exchange wordless glances of dismay. He's come to take us somewhere, and it goes without saying that he could be marching us towards Very Bad Things, and there's nothing we can do about it.

With no choice, we follow him out of the room and down a long hallway. We're both looking around for any clues as to our whereabouts. I see no other servants. We walk in absolute silence, our bare feet sinking into the carpet. There are classical landscape paintings showing hunting scenes on the wall, and sconces with electric lights.

I'm desperately trying to draw reassurance from the fact that we weren't raped last night, that we're dressed in clean clothing. Or is that a bad sign? Is someone trying to make us more presentable before they sell us?

I hate the world I move through these days, a world where I have to search through every kindness, looking for the trap hidden inside it.

Darya's chewing on her lower lip and staring straight ahead with the look of a condemned prisoner marching towards her execution.

My panicked thoughts roll around like tumbleweeds. *Are Simon and Yakov here? Are they dead? Is today the day I die?*

We're ushered into a brightly lit living room. It's decorated in the Russian style, with red Oriental carpets hanging on one of the walls. There are more bookcases at the end of the room, stocked with leather-bound hardcovers in color-coordinated groupings of red, black and brown. Overhead, a crystal chandelier scatters cold white diamonds of light across the hardwood floor. There is a grouping of black leather sofas and chairs set around a coffee table made from a sawed-off tree trunk with a polished top. Sergei, Ludmilla, and Chief Ivanov are sitting there drinking vodka from cut crystal glasses, eating cheese, crackers and caviar from a silver tray, and chatting. How civilized.

My heart twists in my chest, but my face is a blank mask of indifference.

Darya and I walk over and stand there. There are empty chairs, but sitting down with this pack of hyenas would just feel wrong.

Sergei refills his glass, his cold gray gaze fixed on me. He doesn't say a word. And I'm not going to beg him for attention like a love-starved puppy.

So I turn my fury on the chief.

"Why in the hell would you work with someone like

Sergei?" I shout at him. "I suppose you're the roof for his organization?"

"Roof" is a uniquely Russian concept. It means protection. It's a billion-dollar industry here. If you have a business, you need to "buy a roof" from whichever local criminal enterprise is in charge. The bigger your business, the more you need a roof, and the more you pay for that roof.

Chief Ivanov smiles grimly. "No, he's mine."

He sits there and lets that sink in for a moment.

Sergei's the roof.

Sergei's got so much money and influence here that he's providing protection for a police department in a district with hundreds of thousands of people.

In the meantime, Sergei pretends to have little interest in the conversation, draining half his glass in one long gulp.

I spin to face him. "Impressive," I say to him, with venom dripping from my words. "You're still doing well for yourself. So when's the auction, asshole? How much do you think you'll get for me?"

"He's not a trafficker," Ludmilla tells me wearily. She rubs at her face with one hand.

"That's funny. He sure acts like a trafficker," Darya snaps. "What with the kidnapping and drugging us and all that."

"If I were a trafficker, I'd have removed your hair extensions and all the weapons that you have hidden in them," Sergei says to me, ignoring her.

My hand twitches with the urge to pat my hair. *Damn* him. The son of a bitch is always so many steps ahead of me, it's like he circumnavigated the globe and came back up behind me.

"Did you let us escape from that truck on purpose?" I ask him.

"Yes."

The casual admission sends a wave of fury burning through my blood. We were running in terror, freezing, and it was all a game to him.

Sergei, the giant Bengal tiger toying with its prey. I can see a glint of amusement in his eyes.

"You did it so we'd realize that we don't have a friend in the world out here," I spit at him accusingly. "That there's nowhere we can run from you, because everyone is in your pocket."

He inclines his head, his lips curling in a humorless smile. "Something like that."

"So let's pretend you're telling the truth for once in your wretched, pointless life, and you're not a trafficker." I spit the words at him, desperate to hurt him, but he's made of something other than human flesh, and he doesn't even blink. "Then why the hell are we here? Why are they here?" I gesture at the chief and Ludmilla.

Chief Ivanov sets his glass down and leans forward. "Did you girls learn nothing from last night?" His voice is thick with anger. "If we were really traffickers, that would have just been the beginning. Sergei wanted my help getting it through your thick skulls that what you're doing isn't just dangerous, it's deadly. The traffickers in the region are on to your little amateur operation, and there's a price on all of your heads."

I already knew that. What's his point?

Darya spits out an unbelieving laugh. "Excuse me. That was you trying to help us, last night? Including putting a date rape drug in my drink at the bar?"

"That part was real," Sergei interjects, his tone grim.

"He wasn't working for me. You were drugged by a scout for *Cataha*. And we cut the scout's throat."

Darya visibly shudders at that, and hugs herself, sinking back in her seat.

She glances at me. "Natasha saved me," she says defensively. "There was no reason to terrorize her and her friends like that."

Sergei snorts. "*Natasha* is a little girl playing grownup games that are going to end in the deaths of her and all of her friends. So it stops now."

"Do you want to know why the local police department needs a roof?" Ivanov asks.

"Not particularly." My tone is sullen, and I flick a glance at him and look away.

Ivanov stands up and pulls out a manila envelope from inside his jacket. His hand is actually shaking as he opens it and slides out a picture of a nude young woman staring up at the sky. My heart leaps to my throat. She's been slashed from collarbone to navel, her intestines spilling out.

His face is dark with anger. He shoves it in my face, and then Darya's. She tries to look away, but he puts in right in front of her face, inches away. "Look at that!" he barks. "That was my cousin's daughter. She's dead because of my job. Because I'm working with Sergei to take down *Cataha*. Lara was seventeen years old. She snuck out to a nightclub one night, against her parent's orders. That's where they got to her. She was left in the middle of the street in a shopping district, for us to find. After that, I sent my wife and children and my cousin's remaining family, along with my parents, out of the country until *Cataha* is dead and his organization dismantled."

Now I feel horrible. I was assuming the worst of him,

and he's actually risking his life out there and suffering horrific tragedy because of it.

"I'm sorry," I whisper. I look up at him. "But that's what my friends and I are fighting against. How can I sit there in comfort, in safety, knowing that's happening?"

"Because it's not your fucking job to take on *Cataha*, and frankly, you're not very good at it," Sergei snarls at me.

The insult stings, like all his insults do, but I ignore it. "What about my friends?" I ask. "Why aren't they here? What did you do to them?"

Sergei pulls his phone out of his pocket and makes a call. When it's answered, he hands me the phone.

"Simon? Yakov?" I cry out, hope swelling in my heart.

"You're all right?" Simon all but sobs, and I feel as if a thousand-ton weight has lifted off my shoulders.

"I'm fine. Where are you? Can you tell me?"

"I'm back at my apartment. Yakov is with me. Wow, life is interesting." That's a pre-arranged phrase. He's not being coerced.

I relax visibly.

"Brilliant code, there," Sergei observes drily, and I curse myself for being so easy to read.

"The police chief had a talk with us before he dropped us off," Simon says, sounding glum. "I'm sorry, Natasha, we won't be able to do this anymore. We have to shut the whole operation down."

My head is swirling in a sea of confusion. What bizarre kind of angle is Sergei playing here? Why did he choose this method to shut us down?

He could easily have killed us all, if he were a trafficker who wanted to stop us from interfering with him. Nobody would ever have known.

Is the chief telling the truth? Is Sergei?

The chief stands up and looks from me to Darya. "I have to get back to work. If I see either one of you in that nightclub, or any nightclub, I will take you into custody and your ass will sit in a jail cell for the next year. You amateurs have had a few small successes, but your luck will run out sooner rather than later, and these men will rape you with knives until you beg for death, then strangle you with your own intestines." Darya looks horrified. "So if Sergei, Ludmilla and I scared the hell out of you last night and made you think you were going to die, then good. That was just a tiny taste of what to expect if you get caught. Oh, and that video we made you watch, of the woman being hanged? It was legit. We seized that from one of *Cataha*'s men. The woman was a twenty-year-old secretary who worked for the police department. We've never found her body."

I stare at him, and I feel like I'm looking at a truthful man. The lines of anguish cutting into his face, the rage in his eyes – I don't think the best actor in the world could fake that. "I'm sorry. I'm sorry about your cousin, I'm sorry about your secretary. I hope that when you take *Cataha* down, he dies a slow, lingering death."

The chief gestures at Darya. "You're free to leave. I can even give you a ride home if you like."

Darya flicks him a glance of disgust, as if he's a bug that's crawled out from under a rock. "What about her?" She inclines her head at me.

"I need to talk to her," Sergei says.

The butler walks across the room, holding out a coat, which he offers to Darya. It's not the cheap, shabby coat she was wearing last night. It's a beautiful, luxurious brown mink. In his other hand, he's holding out a purse. A Fendi. I'd wager it's genuine.

Darya doesn't take the bait. She shakes her head. "No. I will leave when she leaves."

"You can go," I tell her. "I don't mind."

She folds her arms across her ample chest. "I can, but I won't. You risked your life to save me. I won't leave you with this piece of crap."

Sergei stands up, his eyes blazing with anger. "This is my house, you idiot. I can just have you picked up and thrown out on your ass," he snaps at her.

"Will you please let her stay for now?" I say, forcing myself to be far more civil than I feel. I want her to be free, and safe, and I'm ninety-five percent sure that the chief is telling the truth, but after what happened to us last night, I can't be a hundred percent.

"Since you asked nicely. For now," Sergei concedes. The butler retreats to the back of the room.

Chief Ivanov leaves without a backward glance.

Ludmilla stands up to go too, smoothing out the wrinkles in her dark woolen dress. "I am truly sorry about last night," she says to me, "but Sergei asked me for help in impressing on you the seriousness of your situation, and I owe him many favors. And he's right – it's getting riskier out there, with every rescue that you stage."

"Yes, and it's my life to risk," I snap at her. "My choice."

"It's not your choice, believe me," Sergei says coldly.

I shoot a look at Sergei. "By the way, I think it's beautiful that you and your wife work together so well."

"Wife?" Ludmilla echoes, dumbfounded. "You think I'm married to him?"

"Oh, so I guess it's a different Ludmilla that you're married to?" I ask Sergei.

I still can't believe he told me he was married. That he

was so desperate to get rid of me that he'd tell me such a horrible, horrible lie.

All the computer hacking and research I've done since I've been here tells me that he's not married. And neither is Ludmilla.

Sergei doesn't apologize. He just cocks an eyebrow. "Speaking of creative fiction, does Ludmilla really think that your name is Natasha, or does she know that you're a Toporov?"

Instantly, the temperature in the room drops fifty degrees.

"She's a what?" Ludmilla screeches, spinning to fix me with a look of pure hatred.

"Why would that matter?" I ask uneasily.

"Why would it matter that you lied to me about who you are?"

Darya's gaze is bouncing back and forth between the two of us.

"I have a fake ID and a fake name, yes," I say, confused. Why is she so angry all of a sudden? "So do lots of people in this business."

Ludmilla's face contorts with rage and flushes an alarming red. "Why would it matter that I've been working with the daughter of the man who took my sister?"

CHAPTER FIVE

A lance of anguish stabs me right through the heart.

I knew that her sister had been taken. I didn't know that my father was the one who took her. The misery spread by my family is never-ending. How many lives have the Toporovs ruined?

Her hand shoots out, and she slaps me across the face so hard my ears ring. I stagger back, clutching at my stinging cheek. "You lying bitch!" she screams.

The room explodes in motion.

Darya goes flying at her and hauls her off before she can punch me. Sergei lets out a guttural roar of fury and grabs Ludmilla by the throat.

I jump on him and claw at his hands. "Let go of her! Let go!" I scream. He squeezes until her face turns purple, then releases his grip.

Her mouth is opening and closing like a flopping fish's on a deck, her eyes bloodshot and bulging. She makes wheezing sounds, struggling for words. She backs away from him, stumbles, and catches herself.

"Get out before I kill you!" he shouts.

It's insane. I am falling right back into the *Alice in Wonderland* rabbit hole that is my life when I'm with Sergei. Does he want to destroy me or save me? He just acted as if he'd literally kill for me – after having me and my friends kidnapped and terrorized for hours.

Ludmilla runs out of the room, tears leaking from her pale blue eyes, still gasping and wheezing for air. The butler just stands there as she stumbles past him, as if this kind of thing happens every day.

"What the hell was that?" I demand furiously of Sergei.

"That bitch laid her hands on you, and she's lucky she's still breathing, that's what it was. We need to talk." He glances at Darya. "You need to leave. My men will drop you off."

"Where, exactly, should I go?" she cries out, throwing her hands up in despair. "I have no money, I have no job. I was sleeping in the living room of a flat five blocks away from Club Hollywood. You think I'm safe going back there?'"

Then she looks at me, her blue eyes intense. "You're fighting traffickers? I want in."

"She's not fighting traffickers anymore," Sergei snaps. "She just retired."

I sigh. I haven't retired, but I'm going to have to figure out a new approach, and after what happened last night, I don't feel right dragging anyone else into this mess.

"Darya, Sergei may be an asshole, a liar, a manipulative bastard, and a psychopath..." I glare at him. He nods in agreement. "But he is right about how dangerous it is. You saw that video. That picture. They'll kill you."

"Don't you get it? They'll kill me anyway!" she cries out, her eyes full of tears. "This is the *second time* I've almost been kidnapped by *Cataha*, and the last time, he shot me! How long do you think it will be until the third time?"

She yanks up her T-shirt, and I see two round, puckered white scars on her perfect, flat abdomen.

"Oh God," I say, staring at them. "I'm sorry."

She drops her shirt, and her shoulders sag.

"Last summer, before he started wearing a mask, *Cataha* kidnapped me and a bunch of other girls, and I openly defied him in front of them. He was so angry at me that he shot me in the stomach. Then the police raided him, and it's the only reason I didn't die. I was in the hospital for weeks. I got some money from an organization that works with victims of trafficking, but the money ran out. I couldn't work; I have anxiety attacks all the time. Medication helped a little, but then I couldn't afford to pay for it."

She's staring off into space now, talking more to herself than to us. I don't interrupt. She needs to get this out. She deserves to be heard.

"I ended up sleeping on my friend's couch, and I met this guy who works at a garage down the street, and he was so nice to me. He never pushed me for anything. Grigor. We would just meet up for coffee and sit there and talk. I started feeling better about myself. When I went to Club Hollywood, I even told the bouncer about him, and he said he would buy me a drink to toast my luck, meeting such a nice guy." She laughs bitterly. "Well, forget that. Forget love, forget living my life. I can never feel safe as long as *Cataha* is alive."

"I could give you money to move to Moscow," I suggest. Moscow is almost a twelve-hour drive from where we are. Crime bosses tend to stick to one territory. I don't think she'll be in danger from *Cataha* there.

She shakes her head vigorously, slapping her hands on

her knees in frustration. "No, damn it! What about all the other girls like me?"

She's right. I can't argue with that.

Sergei lets out a growl of impatience. "I'm done arguing. Darya, I will make you a deal. I will ask Ludmilla if you can work with her at *Reforma*, interviewing trafficking victims. I will set you up in an apartment in St. Petersburg, so you can get out of this district and far away from *Cataha* and his men. You'll be in a building in a good neighborhood, with good security. Take the offer, or I'll throw your ass out on the street."

That's Sergei. Mr. Charm.

"You think Ludmilla will work with you ever again after what you just did to her?" Darya asks in disbelief.

Sergei flashes her a grim smile. "I can be extremely persuasive, I assure you. In the meantime, I am going to have you shown to a guest room, because *Natasha* and I need to talk."

The butler leads her away.

I wait until she's gone, then I grab the vodka bottle from the fancy coffee table and hurl it at Sergei. He slaps it aside and it bounces on the rug.

"Hello, Willow. I've missed you." He flashes me that infuriating smile of his. Like all the pain and misery and humiliation he's put me through are a big joke to him.

A red tidal wave of rage floods through me, and I grab a fork from the table and lunge at him, screaming without words.

He catches my wrists and holds them.

"Liar! Pimp! Bastard!" I shriek. Tears run down my cheeks.

He moves and effortlessly pins me down on the couch. "I am only two of those," he says. He straddles me, pinning my hands over my head, and he's as hard as a rock.

"You told me you were a trafficker!"

"Yes. And I lied, because I did not want you to follow me here. I was trying to save you from your own stubborn, stupid, misguided self."

I writhe madly underneath him, and I'm horrified to realize that I'm panting not just with effort, but with desire. The familiar pulse of yearning throbs between my legs. "Let me the fuck up!"

"Giving orders? To me? That's not how this works between us, Willow."

"There is no us!" I scream so loudly my voice is hoarse.

He brushes my hair from my face with his free hand. "Then why did you come after me? I know you've been looking for me ever since you got here!"

His rock-hard cock presses into my stomach. I ram my knees against his back. "Because you lied to me and broke my heart and made me doubt my own sanity! And I needed to know just how incredibly stupid I was for trusting you. I deserve to know the fucking truth!"

"I lied to protect you. Being here, being with me, paints a target on your back."

I try to arch my hips to force him off me, but somehow I just end up moving my crotch right up against his. Mistake. I feel his cock jerk in response. My whole body is humming with desire now.

"Stop fighting me," he says calmly.

I go rigid. "Yeah, you like that too much, don't you? I just won't move at all, then. Until you get bored and let me the hell *go*."

He slides his other hand under my waistband.

"I'll make you a deal. If you really don't want me, if

you're not wet, I'll let you go right now. I'll give you a ride anywhere you want."

"Bastard!" I scream as his hand dips lower and he slides his fingers between my pussy lips.

I'm drenched, and I cannot stop my treacherous body from reacting. I suck in a gasp of pleasure as he moves his fingers back and forth.

"What was that?" he taunts me, and moves down to nip my neck. "I didn't quite hear you."

"I said...let me..." the word I need is "go", but I cannot make myself say it. He's pushing my pants off even as I writhe and fight.

He begins kissing his way down my neck, then bites my nipple through my shirt.

"Oh," I moan, helpless with desire.

"I've thought about you every minute of every day since I left you," he tells me. He pulls up my shirt and kisses my stomach. "I haven't been with another woman. And you haven't been with another man. If you had, I'd have killed him."

"Let me...go..." I force the words out, choking on them.

"Really?" He releases my hands, stands up, stripping his shirt off. My eyes are drawn to his broad torso, scarred with bullet wounds and knife slashes. His flat belly, the perfectly carved square of his six pack. The dark line of hair leading downward from his navel.

"You sure about that?" He drops his pants and underwear in one smooth motion, and his enormous cock is jutting straight up at the ceiling, with a gleaming pearl of pre-cum on the tip.

I can't answer. I struggle to drag the words up from somewhere, but all I can do is stare at him as he slides my pants off.

He bends down and kisses my stomach, then runs his tongue along the outer seam of my pussy.

"Tell me to stop, and I will." He engulfs my clit in his mouth, and I let out a strangled scream. If he stopped right now, I'd murder him.

I don't forgive him, I hate him, I'm furious with him, but right now I'm limp and helpless beneath his tormenting mouth.

Heat pools inside my lower belly, and I part my thighs for him. His hot, hungry mouth closes over my clit and he sucks as if it's sweet candy. He varies the pressure, sending thrill after thrill of pleasure up through my body.

Then he stops. "Tell me you missed this," he commands me, and his hot breath fans my bare, shaved sex.

"I missed this," I moan, tears of humiliation leaking onto my cheeks.

"I missed it too. Yours is the only face I see when I jerk off." I hear the crinkle of a condom wrapper.

He moves up higher until he's on top of me, the head of his cock nudging my entrance.

"Look at me. Look me in the eye." He's never had me look at him during sex before.

I'm helpless. I stare up at him, panting with lust, as he forces himself partway in to me.

The look in his eyes is infinitely tender and loving, and I can't stop crying. My body is shaking with sobs, but I'm still burning up from the inside out with my need for release. I grab his hips, the first time I've ever done that, and pull him into me. He lets out a sigh of pleasure. He's in all the way. I sob as he moves his hips, thrusting in and out, and I keep crying as the pleasure inside me builds and builds until I crash over the edge. I cry as he's coming, groaning, still looking at me as if he really loves me, as if he didn't casually destroy my life last year.

He's still inside me as he lies down next to me and pulls me up against him, and I sob into his shoulder, hating him and loving him so much that I want to die there in his arms.

CHAPTER SIX

CATAHA

Cataha sits in his brightly lit office, leaning back in his chair, pants around his ankles.

This should be a good day for him. Sales are strong, and he's got a sobbing, terrified blonde crawling across the room towards him, slowly, dragging a ball and chain that he's affixed to her slender ankle. She's naked, and her tits are natural, which is nice. They bob with every frantic jerk forward.

But he's just lost a scout, and he's pissed. That asshole Chief Ivanov is going to be sniffing around Club Hollywood now, and that was one of his best sources of hot pieces of ass to sell. Not many virgins, but definitely hot.

Not only that, but it seems as if that fucker Sergei Volkov is somehow involved in this situation.

But there's something else nagging at him. A face from the past.

His men have showed him surveillance pictures from the club. The brunette with the hair extensions...could it be who he thinks it is? It would be an astounding coincidence – but the resemblance is remarkable.

He must know. If it's her, then he must retrieve her at once. She belongs to him.

It will be hard, because that asshole Sergei has excellent security these days, but there's always a way. *Cataha* spent years lying low, playing the nice businessman, planning his ascent. Now he's at the top of the heap in the trafficking business, and nobody will ever displace him again. If he can take out Sergei and grab that brunette bitch of his at the same time, all the better.

No, don't do it. Leave her alone. A high, keening voice throbs in his head. A voice only he can hear.

The voice has changed lately. She used to sing him to sleep. Now she's grown cruel and shrill. He hates her. She isn't real. She's dead. She's gone. She's nobody.

Leave her alone. Leave her alone!

"Shut up! Stop!" he bellows, furious.

The blonde stops crawling and stares at him, eyes huge with fright.

He glares at her and taps his watch. "Not you, slut! Tick, tock. Ten more seconds, or I'll feed you to my dogs."

"No! Please!" She pants with effort as she crawls, dragging the chain, sobbing, and makes it to him just in time.

He grabs a fistful of her hair and yanks her head back hard enough to make her scream in pain. Holding her head still, he slaps her across the face so hard she screams again.

Then he shoves his dick down her throat, choking off her cries. The sound of her panicked gagging fills him with pleasure. For a couple of minutes, as she frantically slurps and sucks, he manages to lose himself in the joy of her debasement. Her ass bears the broad red stripes of his belt. Oh, how he made her dance earlier.

Tears are dripping down her cheeks and splashing on his shoes as her head bobs. She's sucking as if her life depends on it, tongue swirling madly. Finally, he explodes, forcing his cock all the way down her throat until his balls are slapping her chin as she flails in panic.

He slides out of her mouth after she's swallowed every last drop, and she gulps and heaves, kneeling submissively by his feet. He bends down and unlocks the chain from her ankle.

"Peter!" he calls out, and one of his men pokes his head in the door.

"You guys can have her now. Just record it. I want to watch."

She shrieks in horror and clutches his ankles. "Please!" she wails. "You said I could stay with you if I did what you asked!"

"Yeah, you crawled across the room like a good little whore and sucked my dick, but you weren't very good at it." *Cataha* shrugs. "Hey, I didn't feed you to my dogs, did I? Not today, anyway."

Peter hauls her to her feet. He bends her arm behind her back and marches her out of the room, ignoring her sobs of protest.

Cataha stands up and zips his pants shut, and reaches for the phone. He needs to put the orders out to find out the identity of the brunette, and make plans to—

Stop! No! Leave her alone, leave her alone! Coward! Filth!

With a scream of rage, Cataha throws his phone across the room and pounds his fist on the desk. He punches the side of his head, trying to shake the voice loose.

And now his fucking *phone* is broken!

He storms out of the room. He just needs a fresh new

plaything to torment for a few hours. That will take his mind off things. It always does.

Leave her alone, leave her alone, leave her alone!

Cataha's howls of fury ring off the concrete walls, and after he's gone, his men exchange uneasy glances.

Day one...
WILLOW

As I wake up, I realize that my whole body aches, but in a pleasant, delicious way. Sergei hand-fed me dinner last night, while Darya was being whisked away to her new life in St. Petersburg. And when I tried to argue and feed myself, he bent me over the table and spanked me, hard. Then he spent hours alternating between spanking me, fucking me, kissing me, and tasting me everywhere. He was like a man feasting after being starved.

And then, when I was limp and dazed with pleasure, he scooped me up in his arms carried me to his room. His bedroom. He let me sleep in his bed. He never does that. I fell asleep with his arms wrapped around me.

When I sit up, I look around and realize that I'm in bed alone. It's an enormous four-poster with hand-carved columns. The furniture in the room matches the bed, heavy hand-carved wood with a classical look to it. The room is a long rectangle, with a sofa in the middle and a desk, chairs, and book cases on the other end.

I see that he's sleeping on the sofa, wearing boxers and nothing else. Sergei has terrible nightmares, and he's afraid he'll hurt me if he actually sleeps in the same bed with me.

I take a deep breath and summon up my willpower.

So what if sex with him is so amazing that I lose my mind? So what if he's letting me sleep in his bedroom? I'm his prisoner. Again. And I'm done with this. He can't send me away and then reel me back in whenever the mood strikes. And I can't forgive him for how he ended things between us last summer. The cruel things he said to me, every word slashing and scarring like a glowing hot knife's edge drawn across my heart. And what followed after. The weeks of crying, the dull pain that's taken up permanent residence inside my tired, battered soul.

I shove the covers aside impatiently and head to the bathroom. "The bathroom window's not locked," Sergei's voice calls out to me. "Do you want to know why?"

So he isn't sleeping.

I turn and look at him. "Because you've got guards outside?"

"I've got guards. I've got dogs. I've got cameras. Barbed wire. Landmines."

"You do not!" I stare at him. I can't read his expression. Does he?

"Try it and see."

"Yeah, whatever, I'll keep that in mind. And after this shower, we're going to talk. And you're going to explain yourself."

Sergei has never done well with taking orders. He sits bolt upright and fixes me with a look that's supposed to scare me. "Try that again?"

I glare at him. "Why? You heard me the first time. After everything you did to me, I'm through being nice."

I march into the bathroom and slam the door behind me.

After I use the toilet, I get in the shower.

A minute later he joins me.

He pushes me up against the wall. He's naked – and holding a silk tie.

He loops my arms up over the shower head and ties my wrists. I don't fight back – because he'd win, and because my body is already melting with pleasure.

He washes me slowly, intimately. Running the warm soapy sponge over my entire body, massaging my breasts, sliding it between my legs.

Then he washes himself while I watch. I stare unashamed as he washes his cock, the water gleaming off it as it juts up straight and proud.

Then he unties me – and gets out of the shower without a word. Without touching me.

Without fucking me.

I bite back a curse and follow him.

He's not having sex with me because he loves to make me burn for it. And he's punishing me for talking back to him.

In the past, when he made me wait, I let it drive me crazy, but now I have learned to compartmentalize. I've had to. To survive, I've had to take the pain of Sergei's betrayal and wrap it up and shove it into the darkest recesses of my mind.

I can feel a dull throbbing of need between my legs, but I won't give in. Without a word, I dry myself, towel off my hair and get dressed in the light, floating white cotton dress and white sandals he's set out for me on the bed. He's still making damn sure I can't go anywhere. We're in the middle of the frozen spring in Russia, and he's dressing me in gossamer and candy floss.

As I finish getting dressed, he emerges from a giant

walk-in closet, wearing dress slacks and a steel-gray silk shirt.

"Talk to me," I demand. "I need answers about...everything. Why you did what you did to me. How long you think you're going to keep me here against my will."

He arches an eyebrow as he buttons his cuffs. "Are you here against your will? I seem to recall somebody screaming 'please don't stop,' and 'harder' a whole lot last night."

"Yeah, that was fun. Thanks for the orgasms. I'm leaving now. Give me back my coat and purse, and call me a cab."

"Nope." He's walking towards the bedroom door.

Sometimes I could literally murder him. This is one of those times.

"I want answers!" I scream at him, my fists balling in rage. My face flushes, and it takes all my self-control not to fly at him and claw at his face.

"After we eat breakfast." He's completely unmoved by my outburst. "And you will eat all the food that's put in front of you. You've lost weight." He's moving down the hall, and I have to hurry to keep up.

"Do you have to be such a control freak about everything?"

"Do you have to ask?" he parries. "I mean, really, Willow, how long have you known me?"

"Too long." We've reached the dining room. He turns back to look at me.

"Keep it up," he smiles, and a gleam of challenge sparks in his eyes. The promise of future punishment. And I feel a pulsing between my legs, a hunger.

Why does he have to be so perfect and so terrible for me at the same time?

The mahogany table is exquisitely set with a lace table

runner, cut crystal vases with fresh flowers, and hand-painted Wedgewood china. The silver carafe of coffee, sitting on a silver tray, has a laurel leaf motif.

Silence fills the room, as he makes me wait to speak until after we've eaten our omelets, our blinis, and our freshly cut fruit.

Finally he pushes his plate away and nods at me.

"Go ahead."

Fucking controlling son of a bitch.

"What was a lie and what was the truth?" I demand from him.

He meets my gaze. "I am not a trafficker. And I have never been married. Telling you that was the hardest thing I've ever done, but I needed to make absolutely sure that you wouldn't try to follow me."

"Look how well that worked out."

He rakes me with a look of pure contempt. "You're a stubborn fool. You could have volunteered for an anti-trafficking organization, donated—"

I wave my hand to cut him off. "There are plenty of people willing to do that. There aren't many willing to get out in the trenches. I've saved some girls. That means a lot to me."

"Willow the savior," he mocks me. "Do you want to stroke your ego, or do you want to leave this to someone who can make an actual difference in this district?"

"Oh, my God. Sometimes, for just a microsecond, I forget what a total dick you are. Thanks for reminding me." I glare at him. "Every one of those girls who is safe at home instead of being raped, whipped, and murdered...that means nothing to you?"

Sergei snorts in contempt. "Unlike you, I actually think

things through. I play the long game. The most effective
way to end trafficking in this region is to get rid of the head
of the organization. What did Ludmilla tell you about me
and what I'm doing here?"

I scowl at that. "Nothing. She was very closed mouth
about who she knew. I found out you guys weren't married
by hacking into her laptop and looking through her
computer at her apartment."

"Well, aren't you clever." Sergei refreshes his coffee.

"Not clever enough to avoid falling for a psychotic lying
pimping asshole."

"Ah, so you did fall for me. Thank you, that warms
my heart."

Furious, I throw my lukewarm coffee in his face. And
he smiles as he picks up a napkin to mop it up. He's the ice-
man. Nothing rattles him.

"Good girl. I always like it when you give me a reason to
beat your ass until it burns. Not that I need a reason, but it's
somehow more fun that way. Now, let me explain why I left
you and came back to Russia. Why I drove you away. If
you've been studying trafficking in the Pevlova Oblast, then
I assume that you know that last August, right before I left
you, there was an enormous raid in this region. My men and
I were responsible for that. We didn't just free a bunch of
girls. We took down the politicians and cops who were
enabling the operation. The old mayor, the former police
chief, and a number of his men – they're all either dead or
in prison now. They were the last men on my list."

"The list of men who...abused you and your brother?"

He nods, his expression gone grim. "Yes. They were
both on your father's payroll when he was operating in this
area, taking his filthy money to look the other way. And

sampling his wares. They liked to visit the house of little girls."

My breakfast suddenly rises in my throat, and I make a gagging sound. I can never forget that my own father not only trafficked women, he trafficked children as well.

My father. The man who contributed half my DNA. I can't escape the pollution that runs through my veins. I'm a toxic waste dump shaped like a person.

"Sorry," Sergei says. Then he shakes his head. "No, actually, I'm not sorry. You need to understand the depth of evil that you're dealing with here. Running around casually like it's some kind of game."

"I'm not casual about it!" I snap.

He ignores me. "Taking down all those men after I killed your uncle...that was the pinnacle. The culmination of my master plan."

"If that's true, it's amazing." I hope so much that it's true. I don't want to believe that Sergei is pure evil.

He doesn't take the compliment. He shakes his head angrily. "No, Willow, it isn't. The girls that we freed...we didn't do it because we're good guys. We did it for revenge, and no other reason. Freeing all those women cost the traffickers millions of dollars and ended their operations. It was pure selfishness." Then his expression softens. "But you said something that meant the world to me. It made me want to try to live my life a different way. You told me that in the greater scheme of things, I'd won, because your family had failed to make me evil. I want that to be true. I want to be my own man, not what your family made me. I want to do good in the world, for the sake of doing good and no other reason."

He cups my chin ever so gently and makes me look him in the eye. "I'm trying to act like a good man, a moral man, who does something to make the world a better place. If I get rid of *Cataha*, it won't benefit me at all, but the world will be better without him in it. Sometimes I feel like I'm just playing a part, like an actor studying a play and mouthing the lines. But I'm trying."

"Oh." That's all I can say, but I feel as if a tidal wave of emotion just swamped me and I strangle on a sob. It's all I can do not to burst into hysterical tears, and I don't know if it's from love or gratitude or relief.

When we were in California, I tried so hard to reach him, to break through his walls. I wanted him to see him how I saw him – as a miracle of a man who was still good, despite having been forged in the fires of hell.

And it worked.

Or did it?

Sergei is the puppet master who knows exactly which strings to pull. Is this just another twisted game he's playing with me?

"There's one more thing," Sergei says. "I'm not telling you everything. There's something that...I'm not ready to tell you yet. Someday I will. And I want you to know that, because I want us to be honest with each other from now on."

The feeling of gratitude and hope recedes. More secrets. Will there ever be an end to the secrets? My heart feels like a lead weight in my chest.

"Did you ever act as a pimp or traffic children?" My voice quavers as I ask him, and I'm silently pleading for him to deny it.

"No. Never," he says calmly. "The thought disgusts me. The only time I've even done business with traffickers is when I planned to bring them down. And I did, every time."

"Were you married?"

"Never."

"Is Lukas your son?"

"No. He is not related to me in any way. I have no children."

"Then who is he? Why do you take care of him?"

There's a flicker of something dark in his gaze. "I'm not ready to tell you that. I'm sorry."

He's sorry? He can't possibly be as sorry as I have been for the last eight months of misery and crippling self-doubt.

What is the truth? If I can't tell when Sergei's telling me the truth, can I ever trust anyone?

I shudder and twist away from him, and the world feels wavery and strange. When I trusted Sergei, he was my anchor. Now I've been cut adrift and I'm floating away on an endless sea, and there's no safe harbor anywhere, not in the whole wide world.

"What?" he asks.

I slam my fists down on the table and look up again, scorching him with a look of pure hatred. "I'm so angry at you, Sergei! You have no idea how badly you messed with my head! I want to believe you more than anything, and I just can't! Do you realize that I can literally never trust you again?"

He reaches over and his hands gather around mine, squeezing them ever so gently. They wrap around my clenched fists like a blanket, like love, like safety.

"Someday you will. And you will understand that I did it to save you, not to hurt you."

I try to pull my hand away, but he tightens his grip I can't depend on him again. My heart won't survive another blitz attack from Sergei. "Right," I say briskly. "Well, I'd better be on my way, then, so I can get to work forgiving you. Give me a decade or two, and I might come close."

"Don't you understand?" His voice is soft, but it's that tone that lies, it's the velvet wrapped in steel. "I lost you twice. I won't give you up again. You're mine now, and you're never leaving me."

CHAPTER SEVEN

Once upon a time, those words would have meant everything to me. They would have colored my life like a masterful oil painting. They would have filled the yearning, empty spaces inside me, making me feel as if I were finally whole.

From the moment I set eyes on Sergei, I wanted him to claim me. Love me. Protect me.

But now that he finally has – it's much too late.

"How pathetic do you think I am?" I shout at him, so loudly it tears at my throat.

He runs his thumb slowly over the back of my hand. "You're not pathetic at all, Willow. You're strong. You're smart. You're perfect. And you're mine."

Pretty words won't fix this. He's broken what we had. I will not let him shred my heart again; I couldn't survive it. "I fulfilled my end of the bargain," I snap. "The thirty days are long in the past."

He nods. "Yes. And I have come to realize that thirty days would never be enough. I need forever. With you by my side."

I am so furious at this that I rip my hand from his grasp and throw the nearest thing I can grab. A salt shaker. It bounces off his forehead and clatters on the table, and he doesn't even blink.

Because he can hurt me until my heart shrivels and dies, but I can't even scratch his steel surface.

"You son of a bitch!" I leap up and turn to run out of the room, and he's on me like a flash, spinning me around, his massive arms wrapping around me, pulling me up against his massive bulk.

I'm trapped. I kick and claw at his hands, and squirm, but his arms just tighten, pinning me like a butterfly in a collector's glass case.

"You know what happens when you fight me?" he breathes into my ear, his warm breath fanning the flames of my sick desire. "It turns me on. Is that what you want? Shall I fuck you right now?"

Of course that's what I want.

It's what I always want, with him. It never stops. Hot tears burn my eyes and spill down my cheeks.

He can't do this to me. I won't let him! He can't smash me to pieces and leave me crushed and crying...and then casually claim ownership of me, like I'm a pet that he can buy and sell.

"I would have given you anything before!" I cry. "I told you I loved you, and you all but spit in my face!"

He just looks down at me with love and pity. And doesn't let go. "I can tell you why I had to leave you behind," he says. "But it's easier if I show you. Come on, we're going for a ride."

He releases me, and I stumble back, away from him. I hug myself, trying to hold in all the hurt and hate and confusion that's stewing inside me.

"Like hell I'm going with you."

He gives me a look. "Oh, I'm pretty sure you are. You can walk, or I can carry you." He stands there, waiting.

I manage a shaky, hysterical laugh. "You want me to go out dressed like this?"

"I've got clothing waiting for you back in our room." Of course he does. Because Sergei orchestrates every facet of my life. And I didn't miss out on the fact that he said "our" room. He's the lord high king of emotional manipulation.

But as usual, I have no choice in the matter. What Sergei wants, Sergei gets. So I march back to "our" room and dress in thermal underwear, white wool pants, a silk turtleneck, a white cable-knit sweater, and knee-high boots. He grabs a heavy wool coat and knit cap from his closet for himself, and hands me a puffy white down coat.

As the closet door shuts, I see that there's a keypad by the door. He's actually controlling access to the closet. He's the biggest control freak I've ever met.

Sullenly, I follow him to the garage.

"By the way, in case you're wondering if Stockholm Syndrome is setting in yet? It isn't," I snap at him as we climb into a black Bentley in his garage.

"Give it time." His lips curl in a smile as the car pulls out into the cold, white sunlight.

I look out the car window. Sergei's home is a big, ugly red brick monstrosity that doesn't pretend to be anything other than what it is – a compound for a mob boss. There are no decorative columns or shutters to pretty up the house. The windows are barred and the gates are laced with razor-wire. There are guard towers with men watching us as we go.

As we drive, I see that that there are three cars ahead of us, three behind us – and a helicopter hovering overhead.

"A chopper? Really? Bit of a drama queen, aren't we?" I snap at him.

"You'll see," he says.

The rest of the ride is made in silence. We bounce over the potholed road through one of the poorer suburbs of Pevlovagrad, past tiny roadside tea shops and shuttered stores and sagging tin shacks. We glide by graffiti-sprayed walls and empty buildings whose shattered windows seem to watch us like hollowed eyes.

So much poverty here, so much hunger and cold and despair. I understand why girls make foolish choices, why they fall for the traffickers' promises.

Half an hour later, we arrive at our destination – a funeral home.

My stomach clenches in on itself.

He's going to show me more human trafficking victims.

I don't want to see. Why is he doing this to me?

God help me, I already know what a dead, tortured woman looks like. Ludmilla has shown me pictures of *Cataha*'s victims. And Sergei made us watch that video of the woman being hanged. He's already made his point – the traffickers are evil beyond all human reckoning, and trying to stop them is a dangerous pursuit.

A silent man in a dark suit nods at us as we walk through the doors, trailed by a small mob of Sergei's men.

He tries to avoid my gaze. I'm so sick of the corruption and hypocrisy here. I step right in front of him.

"I'm being kidnapped," I say. "I am not here of my own free will. I don't suppose you care, though, do you?"

"Have a nice day, ma'am," he says, nodding politely and moving away from me.

Sergei laughs harshly, pushing me through the lobby. "Did you think that would work?"

"A girl can hope. For the love of God, Sergei, is every-body for sale here in this rotten stinking hellhole?"

"Pretty much." His lip quirks with grim humor. "And if they can't be bought, they can be killed."

He steers me down a hall and into a back room. It's ice cold in here; I can see my breath. The fluorescent lights overhead are blindingly harsh. There's a wall with metal drawers built in.

"What is the point of this? I know what the traffickers do. I've seen dead bodies before," I protest faintly, but it's no good, he's pushing me towards the wall.

"You haven't seen this one," he says coldly, and he grabs the handle and yanks it open, sliding out the drawer.

"Oh, my God!" I cry, and stumble before falling back against Sergei.

It's Maks. *With half his head blown away.*

The other half of his head is perfectly intact. One eye, staring in horror. A mouth gaping open.

"Oh, no," I gasp. "No, no, no."

Poor Maks. I know Maks always hated me, but I never hated him.

I pitied him.

He hated me because of what my family had done to him. My father and uncle owned the whorehouse for little boys where he was raped and abused for months as a child. Sodomized. Made to perform sex acts for food. Beaten, burned, starved.

Unlike Sergei, he let hatred consume him until there was nothing human left. He lived for vengeance and nothing else.

A waste of a life. And now his miserable life has ended.

I'm sobbing so hard I can't speak.

Sergei puts his arm around me and guides me out of the room. He leads me back out of the funeral home, to his car.

As we drive away, he pulls a handkerchief from his coat pocket and hands it to me. I scrub at my face and gradually my sobs quiet.

When we get back to his house, after I shed my coat and surrender it to the butler, Sergei takes me into a media room with a giant TV screen on one wall, and pours both of us a glass of vodka from a well-stocked bar.

Then we sit on overstuffed chairs, facing a fireplace with a crackling fire that I can barely feel.

"What happened to Maks?" I ask, my voice hoarse with sorrow.

Sergei looks straight ahead. I see a muscle jump in his jaw. It's the only indication that Maks' death has touched him at all. "He was driving down the street, in broad daylight, in a shopping district on the border of the Pevlova Oblast. Families everywhere. A group of men pulled up next to him and opened fire. Three bystanders were killed by stray gunfire, and five injured."

"Did the police ever catch them?"

He turns to look at me, his eyes gone winter-gray. "It was the police who killed him. They were in a dark van, but wearing uniforms. They were from the Ruvniya Oblast. The Ruvniya police chief claimed that some of their uniforms had been stolen by thugs, but he lied."

"Isn't it possible that really happened?" I hate suspecting everybody. I hate feeling like there's nowhere safe, no one to turn to.

"Anything's possible." He leans back in his seat, his gloved hands clenching into fists. "But I paid a small fortune to find out the truth, and it turns out that the police chief's brother and two of his top lieutenants took a bribe from *Cataha*."

"So you just had to let it go?" I'm horrified at the thought of those bastards getting away with murdering Maks.

Sergei's laugh is bitter. "Please."

"Right, of course. You killed every last one of the murderers."

"Yes. And that just made it worse. Because now there's a police department only two hours from here that has a target painted on my back. They can come into this district any time they want to. If they try to pull me or my men over and we run, they are justified in shooting us. If we let them take us into custody, we die. That is our life now." He heaves a sigh, his big shoulders rolling. "Here's the problem. Even among criminals, there's a code. You don't renege on your deals, you don't fuck over your partners. And that is exactly what I did when I ran that enormous sting operation on the traffickers last year. Not only that, but I made it very hard for any corrupt police in the area to make a profit anymore. There was a wave of reforms, of raids, dozens of police officers and politicians arrested, and revenue streams turned off. There's so much heat on them now that they're afraid to continue with their trafficking of drugs and guns and humans."

"That's good, though!"

He shrugs. "It's good and bad. It means that literally everybody is gunning for me, and anyone close to me. That's why Maks died. That's what I was trying to save you from. When I decided to go after *Cataha*, I knew there was only one way to save you, and that was to make you stay away from me."

My heart sinks. Then it occurs to me to ask, "Where is Slavik? Did something happen to him too?"

"Recuperating. In Sweden. He went out to buy clothing one day. He was pulled from the store by a mob of *Cataha*'s men and beaten so badly that he was in a coma for a month. While he was comatose in the hospital, a nurse tried to kill him and was only stopped because I had a bodyguard watching him, so I had him flown to hospital in Sweden on a private plane. He'll be back here soon. With dents in his skull and walking with a limp for the rest of his life."

"An assassin dressed as a nurse?" How terrifying.

"No. Worse. A nurse who took a bribe. The bitch is dead now, of course." He looks away. "I sent Kris and Marya to Sweden, too, with Lukas. It's too dangerous for them here."

The thought of someone hurting sweet, gentle Lukas fills me with terror. "Why don't you just leave this area? Go back to America?"

"Why don't you?" he retorts.

I take an enormous swig of vodka before I answer him. "Because I owe a debt of restitution. Because my vile family ruined countless lives, and I have to try to make up for that. I wore designer clothing that was purchased from exploiting child sex slaves. That's a guilt I'll never get over." I shudder and involuntarily rub my arms. I do that often these days – I try to scrub the very memory of those outfits off my skin, sometimes until my skin is red.

"You aren't responsible for what they did. I know I blamed you once. I was a fool."

I set the vodka glass down on a coaster and turn to face him. "I'm not giving up."

He nods. "I know."

Hope flutters inside me. Is it possible? Will he let me

have my life back? "You...you know and you're okay with it? You'll let me go back to trying to save girls?"

Sergei laughs at me. "Oh, absolutely not. You are staying under lock and key until you can look me in the eye and tell me you won't go after any more traffickers. You can work with me in the meantime, you can write articles for the anti-trafficking website that I run, you can do office work for them, but that's it."

I huff out an exasperated breath and turn away. It's infuriating that Sergei is still running my life. I'm not a child, I'm not a slave. I should be able to do whatever the hell I want.

But fighting with him, deliberately defying him, is the wrong way to go about this.

Finally I look back at him, meeting his eyes. "Fine. I won't pursue traffickers anymore. I'm done, I quit. Okay?"

In response, he grabs me, flips me over his lap, and brings his hand down on my butt cheek, harder than he ever has before.

And again. And again.

The first smack snatches my breath away. In the past, when he spanked me, I thought it hurt. I didn't know what pain was until now.

His blows are vicious, meant to bruise.

I scream in agony with every strike. Every time his hand comes down on my ass cheek, I feel an explosion of fire that hurts so much, it shoots through my entire body. He's hitting hard enough to bruise. I frantically push at his legs, trying to free myself. My legs thrash involuntarily, I writhe and shriek, and he keeps hitting me.

My back arches. I can't control my body.

He pauses after each blow, just enough to let the agony spread like a raging wildfire, before he brings down his hand again. There's a violent explosion of pain every single time, and it's getting worse and worse. He's hitting the places he already hit, and it feels as if my skin's going to split open.

"Please!" I cry out. "Please, stop!"

He hits me four more times, wrenching a wordless, gargling scream of pain from me every time.

Then he lets me go. He's breathing hard, furious. I squirm off his lap and scramble to my feet. Waves of fire radiate through my body, pulsing with every heartbeat.

"Wh– wh– why..." I wail. I struggle for breath, frantically rubbing the throbbing skin of my butt. "Why did you do that to me? How can you say you love me and then hurt me like that?"

"Because you just lied to me!" Sergei roars. He leaps to his feet, and he's standing inches away from me, and I gasp for breath. "I always know when you're lying. And because this isn't a fucking game, Willow! Those men will gang rape you and then carve little pieces off you and feed them to hogs while you watch, until there is nothing of you left. Does that turn you on somehow? Is that what you fucking want?"

I'm crying so hard I'm shaking.

"No!" I scream at him. "It isn't what I want! And I don't want it to happen to anyone else, either, and that's why I'm willing to risk my life! Damn you, Sergei, damn you!"

"Can't you see that I love you, you idiot?" He grabs me by the shoulders, his fingers sinking into my soft flesh. "It's a sick love, it's a terrible love, but I love you with my whole heart and soul, if I even possess such things. I can't live without you. I couldn't live with myself if you were killed. So if I have to keep you under lock and key until the day you die, to protect you from your foolish morals and your noble heart, I will do that."

Oh, my God, I am furious. He's telling me that even after he lied to me and ripped me apart last year, I don't have the right to leave him. He's doing what traffickers do. Stealing a woman, hiding her away from the world, and bending her to his will.

And I'm supposed to believe that he's *not* a trafficker?

"I hate you! I want you to die!" I cry out. It's true, but it's only half the truth, and he knows it.

In answer, he grabs my hair and twines his fingers in it. He tips my head back, forcing me to look at him.

"I know. But you love me too," he murmurs. "And I have always loved you, no matter how hard I tried to fight it. I will never send you away from me again. We will work through this together."

"No, we won't." I claw at his hand, trying to free myself.

"As long as you do what I say, and don't try to escape, I'll treat you like gold," he says. "Try to run away from me again, and you'll be punished." He tightens his grip in my hair until I whimper in pain. "Are we clear?"

"You're hurting me!"

"I know. Are we clear?"

"So I'm just supposed to sit here behind these walls and do nothing?"

"No, you're supposed to start planning our wedding. It's one month from today."

CHAPTER EIGHT

After Sergei drops that bombshell into my lap, he leaves to go get some work done – whatever that work might be. I don't bother to ask him, because I wouldn't necessarily believe the answer.

He also lays out a fresh outfit on the bed, and I change out of my warm layers into a pair of cotton palazzo pants and an off-the-shoulder peasant blouse.

Hours later, I'm sitting there in the living room, holding a book but not reading it.

I'm turning Sergei's words over and over in my mind, tearing them apart, dissecting them. I'm trying to force my situation into a shape that makes sense.

Does Sergei really love me?

He's not a man who says things like that easily. And he has no reason to lie about that.

Do I love him?

Yes. Unfortunately. The thought of living without Sergei fills me with an aching emptiness. I never stopped missing him, even while I hated him for his cruelty. My love is without reason, without sense.

I drop the book onto the couch and start pacing the room as frustration swells and bubbles inside me.

I could say all the reasons that I love him. Because he brings me more pleasure than I ever thought possible. Because he's so protective of me, and I know he'd literally die to protect me. Because even after being raised by parents who were more beast than human, and suffering agonies and losses that would crush the soul from most people, I've seen him do decent, selfless things again and again. Because I just *do*.

None of that matters, though. The rational part of my mind knows that after what Sergei has done to me, after the lies he told me, only a crazy woman would return his love.

So call me crazy.

Did he make me that way? Did my circumstances make me that way?

And does any of that matter? I love Sergei, I shouldn't love Sergei, he has commanded me to marry him.

At the heart of it, the problem is he's still giving me no choice. He's dealing with things the way he always does – steamrolling his way in, demanding instant obedience, threatening dire consequences for any resistance. Ordering me to surrender my heart to him, to make a decision that will change my entire life.

I fling myself back down on the sofa and throw the book across the room. The gesture feels weak, unsatisfying. I really want to be detonating dynamite. My rage and hurt need an outlet.

I need more time. I haven't been allowed to process my feelings about him casting me aside and then snatching me back up again. I still don't completely trust him, and I may never trust him. Sure, all the reasons he gave me sound as if they make sense, but once your lover lies to you, can you ever fully believe in them again?

I don't want to be married to him unless I can move past his betrayal, and so far, I haven't. I can't marry him under these circumstances.

I won't.

I'll find a way out.

As I'm sitting there thinking these rebellious thoughts, the door bangs open and I jump guiltily in my seat, as if Sergei could read my mind.

It's one of his guards. They're all cut from the same mold. Big, blocky men with square jaws and pale, merciless eyes, men who could bench-press a Volkswagen.

He approaches me and hands me a cell phone.

"Your aunt wants to speak to you," he says.

When I take the phone, Anastasia is squealing with excitement.

"You're getting married! You're getting married!"

"Wow, word travels fast." I force myself to sound bright and cheerful. She's married to Jasha now. Pregnant with his baby. And Jasha is still loyal to Sergei. There's no point in pouring my woes into her lap, when there's nothing she could do anyway.

She's finally happy, after a lifetime of abuse, fear and degradation. She's safe, her children are safe. He's a wonderful stepfather to them. And a perfect husband for her. She likes to call me up and tell me how many orgasms Jasha gave her the night before – the only man ever to do so. After all the rape and abuse she endured, she didn't even think it was possible.

If I told her what was happening here, she'd flip out, she'd be hysterical, she'd be fighting with Jasha – and it would be to no avail. She wouldn't have a chance of going up against Sergei, any more than I do.

And Sergei knows all that, which is why he's letting me talk to her.

"Yes, Sergei told Jasha and Jasha told me. I'm not sure if I'll be able to travel, though, with me being a big old pregnant whale. Damn the timing! If I can make it, I will, I promise. You must tell me what you want for a wedding gift, though."

Various snarky answers spring to mind. A bear trap for Sergei? A hand grenade? His and her matching cyanide pills?

"Hold that thought. We're still working things out. Sergei may be rushing things with that announcement." I am sure the guard will tell Sergei I said that. Good.

"I was surprised to hear that you guys got back together," she replied. "And that you forgave him. So he isn't married? I hope you gave him hell! Why did he tell you all that? Was he just scared of how you made him feel?"

"He was scared like a little bitch," I say, shooting the guard a defiant look. He pretends he's not listening. "In fact, I made him cry. And I did give him hell. I will continue to give him hell." I'm being wildly reckless saying things like that, but my desire to hurt Sergei in any way at all rides right over my common sense.

"Well, if my doctor says I can't go, then I want you to have a second wedding, here in the States," she informs me. "Because you deserve to have your family at your wedding. And you guys will come to my baby's christening, of course!"

That follows with a few minutes of chatting about the kids – Yuri just won a science fair competition at school,

Helenka is kicking and punching her way through various colored belts and she's also taken up boxing.

Finally I let her go, feeling an ache of loneliness. I do miss them. They didn't want me to follow Sergei to Russia, and they don't understand why I'm here.

After Sergei dumped me, and after I spent three months lying around the house and steeping in sorrow, I just up and left.

I lied and told them I couldn't stay in that house when it held so many memories of Sergei. Well, that was partly true, but mostly a lie. The truth was, I needed to do something positive with my life or I'd go batshit crazy. I needed to stop being the heartbroken loser mourning over a man who was, I believed, fucking his way across the entire country of Russia and back again. And I needed to rewrite my history. I wouldn't be Willow, the daughter of child-pimping monsters. I would be Willow, the girl who made the world a better place, even if it was just for a few lost souls.

So I told them some vague stories about volunteering at an anti-trafficking organization in Russia, and that worried them enough. They thought I was just doing office work. They had no idea what I was really doing.

The minute I hang up, the guard snatches the cell phone away from me

Right. I've got no way to call the outside world.

Message delivered.

A little while later, I'm watching television when the guard returns with a shiny red gift box for me. "Sergei wanted me to let you know that he won't be able to join you for dinner because he's working late." He leaves without another word.

Well, well. Look at Sergei telling me about what he's up to instead of leaving me in the dark. He's trying to show that he's changed. Sending me a pretty gift because he's missing dinner. Pretending to be a good fiancé.

At least, I think that's what's happening, until I set the box down on an end table and open it.

There's a butt plug in there, and a tube of lubricant.

And a note.

Someone's going to be crying like a little bitch today, but it's not going to be me. Go to our room immediately, put that inside you, and wait for me. Eat every bite of the dinner that's served to you. Don't make yourself come, or I will show you what pain really feels like.

Fury and disbelief burn through me. He's got to be effing kidding me!

No, of course he isn't.

I crumple up the note and hurl it to the floor. Then I snatch up the box and stomp off to "our" room and slam the door.

He said immediately. And I'm sure he's watching me on some hidden camera. I want to stall. I want to go take a leisurely shower and then read a good book, just to thumb my nose at him, but then he'll punish me twice as hard.

I open the box and take out the plug. It's got a handle on it. It looks as if it's battery operated, and it looks uncomfortably large.

Fear and arousal swirl inside me.

When Sergei takes command of me, it turns me on like nothing I've ever experienced. It sends me to this strange otherworld, where pleasure is pain, where punishment is reward.

If I say no, he'll hurt me really badly.

I have no choice. He'll take me no matter what.

That's what I tell myself as I slowly slide my underwear off, and step out of my slacks.

I open up the tube of lubricant and squeeze some onto the plug.

Am I doing this because I'm afraid of Sergei, or because I want this to happen to me? I can't tell anymore.

Tears of resentment burn in my eyes as I reach behind myself and start working the butt plug in. It's awkward, and painful.

I thought I hated it when Sergei forced the butt plug into me, but this is worse. At least when he held me down and shoved the butt plug inside me, I could tell myself that he'd overpowered me and I had no choice.

He's doing this to humiliate me. To remind me who's in charge, who's always in charge.

And the worst part of it is, I'm so turned on that I'm wet between my legs. My breasts are heavy and throbbing with need.

The plug is fully inside me now, and I tug on my underwear, then my pants. It feels awkward and weird and it hurts. Not agony, but a dull discomfort, a sense of being stretched open wider than is natural.

I'm slowly walking over to the couch when the plug starts vibrating.

I let out a startled shriek. I can't believe this! He *was* watching me the whole time – enjoying it – and he actually turned the butt plug on by remote control.

It's pulsing inside me, vibrating against the inner walls of my butt. It feels obscene, as if I'm being molested by a piece of machinery. And I'm not allowed to take it out.

I spin around, trying to figure out where he's placed the video camera that's spying on me, but it's hopeless.

I won't be able to concentrate on a book or a TV show. Until Sergei chooses to grace me with his presence, all I'm going to be able to think about is the burning, throbbing sensation in my ass and how much I crave the release only he can give me.

I hobble over to the bed and lie face down. An hour passes by. An excruciatingly long hour. The seconds crawl by, impossibly slow. The buzz of the vibrator is loud in my ears.

When the door opens, I gasp in relief – but it's not who I hoped.

A maid wheels in a tray with a covered silver dome on it. She's heavy-set, with hair parted severely down the middle and pulled into a bun, and dressed in a classic black maid's uniform with a white apron. And the dome is steaming.

Dinner. I'd forgotten about dinner.

I stand up, furious, and wait for her to leave, but she just stands there.

"I have been instructed to stay here until you finish your meal," she tells me calmly.

Oh. My God. If I could kill Sergei right now... I cannot believe he's doing this to me.

Can she hear the vibrating buzzing inside me? If I can hear it, I'm sure she can hear it. I'm mortified. My cheeks flame red with embarrassment.

I grab the dome off the tray and hurl it away from me.

I pick the plate up, limp over to the desk and sit down. I am forced to lean forward awkwardly because of the handle protruding from the plug. I'm praying that she'll just stay there by the door, but she walks over and stands there right next to me. She watches intently while I shovel bites into my mouth, finishing a juicy steak and a bowl of buttery mashed potatoes. I barely taste them, I'm so embarrassed and angry.

She doesn't leave until I've finished the last bite. She

picks up the silver plate cover on her way out. As soon as she's gone, I spring to my feet. Sitting down is incredibly uncomfortable.

And the plug never stops vibrating. I keep praying that the batteries will run out, but they don't.

Sergei comes in fifteen minutes later, and he's got that sadistic gleam in his eyes that promises trouble.

I glare at him.

"Hello, sweetheart. Did you enjoy dinner? You seemed to have worked up quite an appetite." He's unbuttoning his shirt as he talks.

I don't take the bait. "Why did you tell Anastasia we're getting married?"

"Because we are. I've already picked out your engagement ring. It will be here tomorrow." He strips the shirt off, tosses it onto a dresser. I've already looked through the drawers; sheets, pillowcases, no clothing, no useful weapons.

I'm shifting from one foot to the other because of the throbbing discomfort. I'm desperate to pull out the butt plug, but it will come out when Sergei says and not a second before. And begging him will just make him stretch out the torment even longer. "You can't force me to marry you."

Sergei laughs at that as his hungry gaze roves over my body. "Of course I can. Hello, I'm Sergei Volkov. I get whatever the fuck I want."

"You want *Cataha* gone, and he's still there," I snap.

Probably not the smartest thing to say to him at this particular moment, but I'm so furious and humiliated and *turned on* that I can't think straight.

He points towards the bed. I walk over there, grimacing.

He follows me. "You know how I always get what I want?" He is perfectly calm. "By being patient. By being strategic. By knowing exactly when is the right time to make a move. That's how I got you. That's how I'll get him."

I lean against the bed, folding my arms across my chest. "Whatever you say. So. A forced marriage. How would that work exactly? The priest comes in, and I say I don't, and he still marries us?"

"The priest that I bring in will do that, yes."

Damn it! I'm sure he's telling the truth. It infuriates me. Is absolutely everything and everyone for sale?

And that damn plug is still vibrating inside me, sending spirals of hot desire corkscrewing up through my body.

"Why..." I stop and draw in a breath. "Why would you want a forced marriage?"

He ignores my question. "Turn around and bend over the bed, princess. Quickly." His voice is a low, husky growl now, and there's an answering stir in my loins.

But this is my future we're talking about now. I'm determined to fight.

"No! Answer me, damn it!"

Instead, he grabs me by the arm and spins me around so that my back is to him. Then his hand closes on the back of my neck and he forces me to bend over.

"You could have been a good girl. You could have done it the easy way," he says gently. A thrill of fear ripples through me. If there's one thing that I've learned about Sergei, it's that his kindness is a steel fist in a velvet glove. The gentler his voice, the harsher the punishment that follows.

He's fumbling with something, and then I hear clicks. He's cuffed my wrists together behind my back.

Then I hear a snap.

"That's my belt," he informs me. "Do you want to tell

me how sorry you are for telling Anastasia that we might not get married?"

"No!" I scream at him, and I try to straighten up, but he puts his hand on my back and pushes me back down again.

The belt snaps down across my butt cheeks, and I cry out, jerking in pain. The thin fabric of my pants does nothing to protect me, and I am still sore from my earlier spanking.

He hits me again, a line of fire criss-crossing the first. "Stop it! Stop!" I plead.

"When I'm ready."

Another harsh, stinging slap burns my flesh, and I strangle on a scream.

"Please! Stop! I'm sorry!" I cry, hating myself for giving in. Oh, God, I'm so weak. So pathetic. But it hurts so much.

"Think about that before you run off at the mouth again." Snap! I shriek, and my legs kick up involuntarily. I try to squirm away from him. I feel as if he's set the skin of my butt on fire.

He grabs my cuffed wrists and holds me in place. And one more smack for good measure. I howl in pain. "Noooo!"

Tears drip down my face as he slides my pants and panties down to my ankles in one smooth move. "I love how stubborn you are. You have no idea how fucking hard it makes me."

Then he slides his fingers in between my legs. Stroking me, spreading my lips apart, rubbing on my swollen, throbbing clitoris.

"Are you ready for me now, baby?"

"Yes," I sob shamefully, "yes." I hear a crinkling sound as he tears open a condom wrapper, and then he rolls it on. There's an urgent, hungry need, a pulsing between my legs.

And when he pushes the thick head of his cock inside me, I push back against him.

"Take out the butt plug...please...."

He ignores me. He grasps my hips, pumping inside me, slowly at first. I'm so full inside, with his cock and the vibrating plug, that I think I'll tear apart, but the pain is sending me over the edge into that netherworld where nothing exists but sensation. Where agony bleeds over into ecstasy.

He picks up the pace, his fingers bruising me, and his balls are slapping against my pussy.

"Yes," I wail. His breath is quickening. I want him to come. I want to *make* him come. I'm moving with him, moaning wordlessly, and then I feel the explosion in my lower belly, flinging sparks throughout my whole body. My inner walls convulse, squeezing him again and again.

He groans aloud, his body shaking with his climax. When he pulls out, he slides the condom off.

Then he finally pulls out the butt plug and sets it on the nightstand, and I moan with relief.

He unsnaps my handcuffs and crawls into bed with me. He kisses my neck. "You want to know why I'd force you to marry me? That's why. Because with me, your no means yes. And because you love it when I force you."

I roll over slowly, gingerly, with my back and my rectum pulsing in pain, and curl up, hugging my legs. I'm furious... because he's right.

CHAPTER NINE

Day two...
SERGEI

Willow sits in the living room, staring at the enormous sparkling ring on her finger. She doesn't have the look that a normal newly engaged woman does – the look of joy and excitement.

She's got the look of an angry condemned prisoner.

That's okay. We're not a normal couple. I am a man who doesn't ask, he takes. I am dealing out good instead of evil for the first time in my life, but some things don't change. I was born to conquer, and Willow is the sweetest prize of all.

Willow is fighting this every step of the way, and I expected her to. I love her inner fire. She makes herself into a battle worth winning.

She'll come around, the way she always does. She's still hurt, still angry, and it will take a while for her to be able to trust me, but I know that she loves me. And I know that no other man would ever satisfy her, love her or protect her like I will.

So what if she thinks she doesn't want to marry me? I don't care at all. I'm giving her what she needs, not what she wants.

This morning, before breakfast, when I presented her with the engagement ring, I didn't say, "Will you marry me"? Because I knew what the answer would be. Instead, I gave her a different choice.

I told her that she would either be wearing a ring on her finger, or she'd be wearing one on her pussy. I would have her strapped down, legs spread out, and her clitoral hood pierced, if she ever took my ring off. And I gave her five seconds to get that ring on her finger.

The look she gave me would have burned the skin off a lesser man. I just stood there, basking in the warmth of her rage, and after she put the ring on her finger, I bent her over the dining room table and knelt down behind her. I tortured her with my tongue and my fingers, taking her to the brink and then pulling back, until she cried and begged me to take her.

Her sweet pleas are my oxygen. My meat and drink. How can she be foolish enough to think I could ever live without them?

When she'd begged enough, I fucked her so hard that the vases on the table fell over, and she screamed my name, pleading with me to go even harder.

After breakfast, I bring in a makeup artist and hair-dresser, and I have her styled like a *Vogue* model and dressed in a floor-length Baliencega gown. Her eyes are smoky, her lips pink and glossy, and her hair is styled in shining waves.

I put on a tuxedo and march her into the drawing room, where a photographer is waiting to take our engagement pictures.

"Got anything to say, sweetheart?" I taunt her, and she stabs me with a murderous gaze.

"I'll just let you do all the talking, since you know everything," she says, through gritted teeth.

We spend half an hour posing for pictures. I have one of my men take some pictures with a cell phone so we'll have them right away. After the photographer leaves, I take Willow into the drawing room, hand her my cell phone, and make her send the pictures to her aunt and, for good measure, to Darya and Ludmilla.

Since she was a good girl, aside from pouting and glaring when she thought I wasn't looking, I let her call Darya, although I'm standing behind her chair and hovering over her the whole time.

I listen to her silly gossip for a few minutes as the two of them chat about St. Petersburg, about Darya's new apartment, about how Darya loves her new job and feels like she's finally doing something worthwhile with her life. Darya is now a paid intern, being trained in multi-media journalism, creating video presentations for *Reforma's* website. In a year they'll put her on staff. I'm financing it.

Willow, ever the sweetheart, begs Darya to send a text to her car mechanic friend, even if it's just to let him down gently. Darya promises to think about it. So much sweetness between these two women, it could rot my teeth. All this *caring* about *feelings*. It's moments like this that remind me that I'll never really know what it is to be human. Being with Willow is as close as I get to experiencing normal human emotions.

As Willow talks, I drop my hands to her shoulders and begin massaging them. Then I bend down and bite her neck, making her gasp.

"Oh, it's nothing!" she cries out to Darya. "I just spilled

my drink on my lap." She tries to stand up, but I press down on her shoulders, holding her down, and I bend down again, nibbling her ear. Willow quickly says goodbye to Darya.

When Willow hangs up, I smile at her. "See what a nice guy I am? Helping out your friends like that?"

She twists around and singes me with a look. "Your dictionary must have a different definition of the word 'nice' than mine does." Her beautiful face is set in an angry mask. "I'm happy Darya is doing well. I'm happy for her that she gets to choose what she wants to do with her life. I wish I had that for myself."

I reply with a cool smile. "Oh, ouch. Your words hurt me so deeply. In fact, I've changed my mind, you're free to go."

"Really," she says, not taking the bait.

"Well, you're free to go change back into your regular clothes. I've got some work to do."

She's muttering rebelliously as she walks away, but I just smile and let her have that. Let her think that she's got some control over her own destiny. I'll have so much fun proving her wrong.

Days three and four...

Willow moves stiffly through the house, refusing to meet my gaze, only speaking when spoken to. She does her best to avoid me; she goes into areas of the house where she thinks I won't find her, like the kitchen, and hangs out there, reading, until I come get her.

She hasn't looked at the stacks of wedding magazines I bought for her. Yes, when I take her to bed, she still comes for me. She more than comes. She cries, she begs for it, she crawls across the bed on command and takes my cock into her mouth. And afterwards, she lets me gather her in my arms and pull her to me, crushing her against my body. She falls asleep in my arms, her breaths deep and even.

But when we're not having sex, she's angry and sullen, and she's so damn stubborn I can see her doing this right up to our wedding day. I could threaten to beat her ass, but we both know that's more pleasure than punishment for her, unless I really hurt her, which I don't want to do.

Finally, I offer to let her leave the house on one condition – she has to agree to have another GPS tracker put in.

And of course she can only leave with me, under armed guard. That last part is as much to keep her alive as it is to keep her from running.

She agrees, with a lot of muttered cursing and resentful looks.

On day five, once she's had the tracker put in, we head out to the Brick Market to go shopping. It's located at the former brick factory, which shuttered its doors ten years ago. When the brick factory went out of business, it threw Pevlovagrad's economy into a tailspin, which is why it was so easy for slime like Willow's father and uncle, and *Cataha*, to move in and start their trafficking businesses.

I offered to take her to a high-end department store, but she asked to go to the Brick Market instead. There are hundreds of little stalls there where people sell everything from dishware to vegetables to clothing. That's just like her. She wants the money to go to the housewives who eke out a living selling scraps, and she'd rather buy used clothing from a little stall, even though she knows I'd fill her closet with designer clothing.

Before we leave I remind her not to try to run away. "I own this town," I tell her. "There would be no point."

She tries to punish me by ignoring my presence and staring out the car window as we drive. That's fine; it gives me time to do some work on my laptop. I'm still running my legitimate business, including a shipping company and several construction companies, at the same time I'm working with the police chief to flush out and destroy *Cataha*.

It's a weekend, and the market is bustling with bargain-hunters. There are booths selling electronics, dishware, books, sheets, furniture. There is a section dedicated to Soviet memorabilia.

First Willow buys sets of *Matryoshka* nesting dolls to send to Yuri and Helenka. Then we shop at a stall where they sell traditionally painted *Khokloma* jars and bowls and table-ware, red and black and gold.

Then Willow has to buy baby clothes for Jasha and Anastasia. After a couple of hours, my butler is laden down with shopping bags. We're just like a normal wealthy couple shopping on a weekend. Except we're anything but that.

But it seems as if this shopping trip is good for her. When she's chatting with the vendors, in excellent Russian with barely a trace of an American accent, the anger and bitterness starts to fade. Her eyes are alight with happiness. I feel the tightness inside me uncoil a little. I want her to look like that all the time.

I am the one who painted that haunted expression on her beautiful face, and it is up to me, my new life's mission, to take it away.

Wanting her to feel free, to be happier, I make the mistake of letting Willow do a little shopping on her own — with my guards trailing ten yards behind her for safety, of course.

Then a stall keeper sidles up to me. He tells me that

Willow secretly offered him money to buy a cell phone. I shake my head in frustration.

This again? How the hell does she think having a phone would help her?

I grab her by the arm and march her towards our car, with our guards closing around us.

"Nice job trying to buy a cell phone," I snap at her.

She doesn't look the least bit abashed.

"Which time?" She meets my gaze defiantly.

Oh, no. My woman does not speak to me like this. She may be as stubborn as a team of mules, but she's not unbreakable. No one is.

"I've been going much too easy on you. That ends now," I snap at her.

I don't even bother to lower my voice.

I'm seriously pissed off that she's trying to escape after I warned her not to. Why is she being such a stubborn fool? Going behind my back like this just makes me look bad.

She is my fiancée, soon to be my wife, and I won't tolerate this kind of behavior. When we get home, her punishment won't end in orgasms. It will end in screams.

"So literally everybody in this town is in your pocket." Her tone is disgusted as I shove her into the car.

I settle in next to her. "You see this marketplace, all the people here? That's all because of me, which means I provide a living for hundreds of people. I paid to promote it, I took it from nothing to success in just a few months. People here are loyal to me because their livelihood depends on it."

"You're such a philanthropist. Really, I feel honored to know you."

"Keep talking," I growl at her. "You're digging your own grave with your mouth."

CHAPTER TEN

Day five...

WILLOW

I won't even look at him as we pull away from the Brick Market.

I'm furious. And he doesn't understand at all.

One way or another, I will find a way to get out of this wedding. I still don't know if I can ever trust him again, but if I'm going to be married to him, it must be my choice, not his.

He's brilliant in so many ways – but not in matters of the human heart. That's because he had to guard his own heart like a fortress, had to tell himself he didn't have one, in order to survive his early life and then to carry out his mission of revenge.

I know he's going to punish me brutally when we get home, and I'm afraid, but I'm not sorry I stood up to him. I'm relieved when I see that we're pulling into a parking lot with a row of stores in it, because it delays the pain for a little while at least.

When we park, Sergei's men park next to us, and he

waits until they've all poured out of their cars and scanned the parking lot before we get out of his car. How bizarre we must look, on this normal day, in this normal place.

There are families strolling through the parking lot, and I look at them as Sergei pushes me along.

"This is what people do, Willow. They marry, they have children, they dedicate their lives to each other. See how happy they are?" He gestures at them impatiently.

That isn't us. Our life looks nothing like that.

"Yeah, I'd be willing to bet money that's because all those women had a choice when they said yes." I glare up at him.

I see his eyes spark with anger. I could pretend to go along with this charade, but why bother? He'd know I'm lying.

He puts his hand on my back and propels me towards the sidewalk.

Does he really think that we could ever have what these people have?

The mystery of why we stopped here is solved quickly. We pass several stores and end up in front of one that specializes in wedding cakes. He marches me through the door, and his men line up outside. Sergei turns the "open" sign around to "closed"; apparently he's booked the entire business for today, just for us.

Model cakes are everywhere, gorgeous, elegant, set with edible pearls and bows, shaped like mansions, like castles, like a giant swan with a couple riding on its back. There are cakes that look like flower gardens, cakes that are set up like an entire landscape with trees and ponds and fountains.

The baker, a rotund man in his fifties, bobs his head eagerly when we come in. Another Sergei sycophant. He babbles congratulations and praise for Sergei.

I'm getting madder and madder.

I cross my arms over my chest, hugging myself, and I'm gripping my arms so tightly that my knuckles are white.

This is not my dream wedding. Looking at those families out in the parking lot didn't make me jealous, it made me furious. And reckless.

When the baker brings out a book of pictures, I shake my head. "Gee, I hope we're not wasting your time. We're not sure of the date yet."

The baker's eyes fly open wide with surprise.

Sergei shoots to his feet. "Leave the room," he says to the man.

The baker starts to say something, then takes one look at Sergei and literally runs out of the room through the back door.

Sergei bends my arm behind my back and forces me to bend over, my face pressed against the plastic pages of the wedding cake book. "We're very sure of the date," he growls.

He grabs my waistband and slides it down. My pants fall down around my ankles. I'm naked from the waist down. I struggle, and he bends my arm up more until pain forks through my body and I'm forced to hold still.

"What are you doing?" I cry.

"Claiming my bride. Right here. Every time you try to say that you're not mine, I will remind you that you are. So think about that if you decide to do it right in the middle of a market, or a department store. I'll bend you over one of the counters while families walk by with their children, and I'll take you up the ass."

"Sergei, no! Not here! Please!" I cry out, mortified. There's a big picture window on the front of the store! Yes, his men are blocking it, but there's the chance that somebody walking by could see us. And the baker is in the back – surely he'll hear us.

"I love it when you say please." His voice is a low, sexy growl. "You should say it more often. I might not have to spank you so hard." I hear cloth rustling. He's sliding his pants off. Then I hear crinkling as he tears open a condom wrapper. Moments later, his cock is pressed against my rear entrance.

"Ass or pussy. I'll let you choose."

Panic rushes through me, and I choke on a sob. "Not my ass. Please." I'm still sore and aching from last night. If he doesn't have lube, and take his time using a butt plug first, it will be agonizing.

"Then say what you want."

I almost scream at him that what I want is for him to leave me the hell alone, but that's not true. All he'd have to do would be to stroke me, to feel the moisture oozing between my legs.

"I want your cock in my pussy," I mutter furiously.

"Louder!"

"Someone might hear me!" I plead. He can't make me do this.

"I hope they do," Sergei growls.

I am mortified. I am crying, tears streaming down my cheeks, splashing onto the plastic pages. *And I am so wet.* I'm panting with desire. My ass is rising up to meet him, back arching.

He presses the head of his cock against my small, puckered, rosy hole, and starts to force his way in. A lance of pain sears through me.

"No," I plead. "Not there!" I gulp, and force myself to yell out loud, "I want your cock in my pussy!"

He repositions himself and forces his cock inside me

without even bothering to stroke me the way he usually does. He doesn't have to. I'm oozing with moisture for him. He rams in hard, holding me firmly by the hips.

Then he takes his time, sliding slowly in and out. Drawing it out. The heat between my legs burns me, it hurts, it screams for release. He can always tell when I'm about to peak, and every time he freezes, mid-stroke.

Finally, I pant, "Please, Sergei, please let me come!"

"Are you sorry?" He's still a statue. I try to squirm back against him, but he holds me so that I can't move.

Damn him to the fiery pits of hell!

No, I'm not sorry.

Yes, I'm sorry that I am being dangled over the peak like this, my entire body a throbbing pulse of need.

The words come out without my meaning them to. "Yes, I'm sorry! I'm sorry!" I wail. "Please let me come!"

Then he begins pumping inside me, harder and harder, slamming the table against the wall with his thrusts. When I come, I cry out again, without words this time, as the pleasure crashes over me and leaves me dazed and breathless. I'm shaking and sobbing. I don't know if I've ever felt this humiliated.

Still inside me, Sergei calls out, "You can come in now!"

I let out a strangled scream. He slides his cock out of me, and I frantically pull my pants up.

I'm still zipping my pants when the baker strides back in through the door, smirking. My face is tear-drenched, my makeup no doubt a mudslide down my cheeks. And I know I'll have that sex-swollen, hair-rumpled look that announces exactly what happened here moments ago. To say nothing of the fact that the air reeks of our lovemaking.

Sergei forces me to sit there at the table, in front of the

man who heard me screaming for Sergei's cock. I am bright red with embarrassment; I know because I can feel it.

The baker doesn't say anything about what he just heard, but he keeps smirking and shooting me lascivious looks.

We slowly page through pictures of cakes. I'm ready to pick the first one, but Sergei insists that I look at every single picture in the book. Just when I think the torture has ended, Sergei insists that I have to taste some samples – which he insists on feeding to me.

"Do you like that in your mouth?" he taunts me. The baker's eyes are practically bulging out of his head, and he licks his lips.

When Sergei finally settles on the very first cake we looked at – a traditional three-tiered buttercream cake adorned with red roses – he's smug, and I'm burning with anger and humiliation.

He pays the baker, who can't seem to take his eyes off me.

"Don't you want to thank the nice man for his wonderful service, darling?" Sergei's voice caresses me, mocks me, promises even more punishment if I don't do exactly as I'm told.

"Th-th-thank you very much," I say to the baker. I'm so mortified I have to force each word out.

A leer twists his face. "Oh, it was my absolute pleasure to serve you. Please come back *any time*."

I feel sick at that. Sergei prods me.

"Of course," I mutter.

Finally we're walking towards the door. I never want to set foot in there again.

"So, you defied me, and mouthed off to me in public.

How did that work out for you, sweetheart?" he taunts me as we leave the bakery.

The parking lot is crowded as we start to make our way towards his car.

I don't care. I'm ready to scream. I want to claw him and make him bleed. *How could he do that to me?* I start to curse him out when I hear the screeching of tires, then panicked screams and the splatter of bullets.

One of Sergei's men cries out. *"Cataha!"* he shouts. And then a fine mist of red surrounds his head, and he crumples to the ground.

CHAPTER ELEVEN

Day five...
WILLOW

A mob of people literally pours over me and Sergei, ramming us like panicked bulls, forcing us apart with their sheer mass as he screams curses into the wind.

Women holding children, men pulling their wives, people scrambling for cover, for safety. Gunfire, the smell of blood, the shrill cries of terror and pain. I'm carried away by the crowd, crying out, flailing my arms.

I see a dozen SUVs with dark tinted windows blocking the exits to the parking lot, and men with machine guns spraying Sergei's men with gunfire. Sergei's men are wearing body armor, and they return fire with deadly precision. Bodies drop, blood sprays.

The crowd scatters, and I stagger, looking around wildly. I am choking with panic. I can't see Sergei. There's a child lying on the ground, his blue eyes wide with terror, his mouth open in a wordless wail. I run to him on shaky legs, scoop him up into my arms and stagger towards a concrete column. A woman grabs him from my arms and dashes full speed towards the street, and I hear more gunshots and screams. Men lie crumpled on the concrete, their arms splayed out, their heads exploded like ripe melons. Sergei's men? *Cataha*'s? I can't tell.

Then I see a cluster of ski-masked men with machine guns moving towards us, and I know they're not Sergei's men. A group of shoppers are trapped out in the open. I'm one of them.

We all freeze. There's nowhere to run. I hear pops of gunfire, and I don't know if Sergei is dead or alive.

The thought fills me with mortal terror. It ices over my soul. *Please don't be dead, please don't be dead.*

I hear a child scream in terror. "The devil! The devil!" And my heart stutters in my chest.

It's him. Pushing forward to the front of the group. Bulky body armor, gun in hand, devil mask with curling horns. *Cataha.* And this time I'm sure it's the real one.

Suddenly, a crazy thought occurs to me. I've got a GPS tracker in me again. If *Cataha* took me, Sergei would move heaven and earth to find me, and he could end *Cataha.* The Pevlovagrad Oblast's nightmare would finally be over.

Everyone else is running away now, scattering. I don't run away. I stand stock still, pretending to be a deer frozen in the headlights.

A group of men surround me. One of them grabs my arm and hustles me towards *Cataha.*

He looms over me, a figure torn free from nightmares and let loose in our world. The red and black mask glistens in the cold sunlight.

"What's your name, girl?" he demands, leaning towards me. His voice is raspy, and I think, *It's really him.* I feel sick with fear and hate. When I look at him, I see oceans of blood, I see the eyes of the dying. The ghosts of the murdered are screaming in my ears.

I glare at him. He'll probably kill me, but I'll die fighting. "Well, I can tell you one thing, motherfucker, it's not *girl*."

One of the men smacks the side of my head with the butt of his gun, and I bite down on a cry of pain. Sparks explode behind my eyelids. He raises the gun to hit me again, and *Cataha* rasps, "Stop!" He points his gun at a cowering family who are trapped in the middle of the parking lot. A moon-faced man and his moon-faced wife, hugging their chubby little boy, condemned to death because they ran in the wrong direction. They cry, hugging each other, and the hatred that floods my body threatens to choke me.

"I said, what's your name?" he husks, his terrible voice rasping over each word.

I grit my teeth. "My name is Natasha Vodianova." That is the name on my fake ID.

He cocks his head to the side. "You sure?"

"Am I sure about my *name?*" I snap. "Yes, I was born with it, I've had it my entire life, so I'm pretty confident."

"You're from America. Where in America?"

Damn my accent. I've worked really hard to lose it, and I can frequently pass, these days, but apparently he's not fooled. And I know that American girls are especially prized.

"New York. What the hell does it matter?"

"Bullshit," he rasps. "You don't have a New York accent."

Before I can answer, I hear the pop of bullets, and the man who hit me with the gun staggers. There's a hole in his forehead, and his eyes are rolling back.

Cataha's men scatter. They close in around *Cataha*, shielding him with their bodies.

"Bring her! Bring the girl!" I hear his hoarse screech. There's a hailstorm of gunfire, and I duck and run as fast as I can while half bent over.

I should have let him take me. I should have followed his men. Why am I such a coward?

That would have been too obvious, though, wouldn't it? Wouldn't he have suspected that I have a GPS tracker if I'd just let him take me? I am kneeling, I am dazed and terrified, I don't know what to do or where to go.

A strong hand grabs me, and I scream and flail until I realize it's Sergei. He hauls me up by my arm, throws me into the back seat of a car, and hurls himself in after me. The door slams shut.

"Are you hit?" he demands urgently. I look down and realize with amazement that there's a bullet hole in my coat. No, three bullet holes.

"I don't– I don't– I don't know. I don't think so. I can't feel anything right now."

The car screeches out of the parking lot. I hear a chopper overhead. Other cars are following us. Sirens wail as police and fire trucks rush past us.

"Take your coat off."

I wriggle out of my coat, and he runs his big hands up and down my body until he's satisfied that I'm not injured.

I hug myself, shaking violently. *All those innocent people...* I pull my knees up to my chest.

"I thought you were dead." I can't say the words louder than a whisper, because they're so terrible.

The grim, dirty streets of Pevlovagrad slide by us as we speed away from the scene of carnage at the market.

"And that upset you?" His voice holds a bitterness I've

never heard before. He's sitting right next to me, but he sounds so distant he might as well be on the dark side of the moon.

"Of course it upset me! What do you think I am?" I cry out, shocked. I stare at him in disbelief. His face is set in grim lines, and he looks out the window instead of at me.

"You're the woman who's fighting to get away from me every minute of the day."

Seriously?

"That's...that's...you know why I'm doing that!" I cry out. "You told me you were married to Ludmilla; you told me you were a pimp. You climbed in a plane and flew away, leaving me so devastated I barely got out of bed for weeks. For eight long months, that was my reality. I fell in love with a lying, married pimp. I lived with that sickening feeling in my stomach every minute of every day. And now you expect that I should instantly trust you again?" I fling my hands up in the air in frustration. "You know what? We've had this conversation. I'm not going to go over it again. I am angry at you, and I am hurt, and I don't trust you. But that doesn't mean I want you dead. If anything happened to you..." The thought floods me with such devastating sorrow that I choke on a sob. "I would never get over it."

He turns his wintry gaze back to me. "Do you mean it?"

There's doubt in his voice. I've never seen him show the faintest trace of doubt in any way. I actually believe in him right now, at least about this. He wants reassurance. He wants to know that he matters to me.

My heart hurts at the thought of him wondering if I care whether he lives or dies. No matter how angry I am with him, he can't think that. "Of course I mean it. I don't lie to you, Sergei. I care about you. I want you to be happy. Do you really question that?"

He doesn't answer for what feels like a long, long time. "Sometimes."

"Do you think that you could hurt me so deeply if I didn't love you? Do you think you could make me so very angry and ready to freaking murder you if I didn't care about you to the very depths of my soul?"

At that, he manages a grim laugh. "No. I suppose not."

"Even at the worst moments, even for these many long months that I thought you might actually be a human trafficker, I still loved you. Always." I look him in the eye. He has to know the whole truth. "But if you were a trafficker, if you *are* a trafficker, and if I had a gun...I'd kill you. No matter what my feelings for you are. No matter that it would destroy me. If you were like *Cataha*, I'd kill you. You need to know that about me, Sergei. You need to know what I'm capable of."

He takes my hand in his, gently, as if he's afraid to apply any pressure at all. "That's more than fair, since you've seen what I'm capable of. But you need to know two things. One, I have never been a trafficker, and I only told you that to save your life. And two...*I will never let you go.*"

So you think.

I let him pull me close to him, and I sink into the heated strength of his body.

"How did *Cataha* find us at the market?"

"I'm not exactly low-profile. I can't be. Aside from the fact that I stand out physically, I travel with a large crew. Somebody saw us, called it in, and betrayed us. We're working on finding out who."

"How many men did you lose? How many civilians were killed?"

His tone turns grim and his muscles tense. "Two of my men, six of theirs, and at least four shoppers."

I feel queasy, the slices of wedding cake roiling in my stomach. "I'm sorry for your loss. God, I want that bastard dead so badly."

He shifts in his seat and grabs my chin, forcing me to look at him. "Do you understand the danger now? Why I can't let you go on rescue missions anymore? Damn you! Why are you not afraid?"

Thank God he doesn't know that I almost willingly handed myself over to *Cataha* and his men.

"Of course I'm afraid!" I cry out. "But so are those girls. Girls just like me, snatched from their families, from their lives. My family did that to them, made them suffer unimaginable terrors. And most of those girls ended up dead, and their families never even knew what happened to them. You're not the only one who's tarnished by their past. You're not the only one who needs to do some good in this world, Sergei."

"When I take out *Cataha*, will that be enough for you?" he demands.

I consider that. "I would need to keep working to help take down traffickers."

"Will you ever be content with working behind the scenes?"

"You want an honest answer? Maybe. I don't know."

I look down at my arm, and the air around me swims and turns hazy.

Oh God. It's coming for me again. The sickness.

I see rot and corruption, filth crawling over everything. I pull away from him and start punching the car door again and again.

Sergei grabs my arm. "What are you doing?" he shouts at me. "Do you want to get away from me that badly?"

"Me! Me! I want to get away from me!" The words tear out of my mouth, high-pitched and hysterical.

His fingers tighten around my arm like steel. "Willow, calm down. What just happened?"

"It's my flesh, Sergei." Tears run down my cheeks now. "My polluted, dirty flesh. Sometimes I just have to hit things. I'm filth, do you understand that? I had a teddy bear that came all the way from Russia, when I was a little girl." I'm heaving with sobs. I try to push the memory to the back of my mind, but I can't. "It sat on my windowsill, and I loved it. Its fur was as soft as silk, and it was dressed in a little frilly gown. My father brought it home for me. Can you imagine how many children were raped to pay for that filthy, evil teddy bear?"

Where has all the air gone? I'm gasping and heaving, struggling to breathe. I stare into his eyes, desperately searching for understanding. I want to see disgust there, the disgust that I deserve for being a Toporov.

He should agree with me. He should push me out of the car into the filthy snow and drive away as fast as he can. He should leave me to freeze, to melt into the snow.

I dread these moods, how they swoop down without warning and seize me up in a whirlwind of self-loathing. "Why don't you hate me?" I scream at him, balling up the fist of my free hand and punching my leg as hard as I can. "Why don't I make you sick?"

The outside world has vanished. I feel as if I'm in a suffocating bubble, sucking in toxic fumes that cloud my mind.

He strokes my hair, and his voice has gone tender and soft. "Because you were a little girl who didn't know what your father really was. Because it was never your fault. And because..."

He looks as if he wants to say something else, but he stops himself. He just shakes his head and pulls me into his embrace. He wraps his loving arms around me and holds me tight while I scream and struggle and try to claw at my face. All the while, he's kissing the top of my head and murmuring, "It's all right, it's all right. I'm here, baby. I'll never let you go."

Hysteria bubbles up inside me, and I might be laughing, or I might be crying. "I'm sorry. I'm sorry. I'm sorry."

His strong body is an anchor, holding me close, keeping me from floating away. "Don't be sorry. I'm the last person to get upset at you for letting the darkness take you sometimes. But I'm with you, Willow, always. I won't share you with the darkness, because you're mine, only mine. I won't let you hurt yourself." He kisses the top of my head again, with amazing tenderness.

The darkness starts to fade. Light seeps in. I can feel again, his muscles bunching as he holds me against him, the vibration of the car motor, the frantic flailing of my aching heart.

"That's your job, is it?" My voice comes from far away.

His arms tighten. "I hurt you the way you like it. The way you need. You are punishing yourself when you have done nothing wrong. And I won't allow that. It is my job to protect you, and protect you I will."

CHAPTER TWELVE

Day six...

I spend the rest of the day in a quiet funk. Sergei's in his office, dealing with the aftermath of the attack at the Brick Market. He leaves a bodyguard with me the entire time he's gone, however. I think he's afraid I might hurt myself.

Our dinner together is quiet; we barely speak to each other. He tells me that he's found out the name of the person who called *Cataha* – someone at the market overheard one of the merchants phoning him. He doesn't tell me what he did to the man; he doesn't have to.

I fall asleep in Sergei's bed, wrapped in his arms. He just holds me, stroking me gently, and doesn't say a word.

But when we wake up, everything is back to what passes for normal around here.

After breakfast, Sergei leads me into the drawing room and gestures at several three-ring binders splayed out on the coffee table. Pictures of wedding decorations in one book, wedding dresses in another, and flowers in the third.

"There's a change of plans. We'll be getting married in Sweden," he tells me. "I want Lukas to be able to attend, and your family, and this will be safer. Look through these books and give me some answers."

I refuse to sit down, and I don't even spare the books a glance. I wrap my arms around my waist. "Can you please just *slow down?*" There's a snap of impatience to my voice. "Just give me a few months, at least?"

It's like arguing with a slab of concrete. His expression doesn't even change. "No, I won't. Why should we wait?"

Frustration bubbles up inside me. "Because I need time."

"What would be the point?" His eyes frost over. I'm staring at Winter Sergei again, the one carved of ice, the one I can't touch without burning my hands. "The end result would still be the same. You will marry me. You know that. I know that."

I stiffen with anger. I'm not one of his foot soldiers, to be barked at like a cringing dog. "No, actually, I don't. It's not a marriage unless I say yes. Not a real marriage. And I haven't said yes."

"This again?" His voice has a dangerous edge to it now.

"Again. Still. Forever."

I turn away from him. If I'm ever to forgive him, if I'm ever to agree to marry him, it can't be under duress. If he doesn't let me make up my own mind, I will spend the rest of my life waiting for the time when I can bolt, and sooner or later, even if it takes years, that time will come.

Sergei's right about one thing.

When it comes to getting what you want, timing is everything.

I look up at him, shivering a little at the chill I feel radiating off him now. "Who is Lukas, and why are you caring for him? What is the secret you're not telling me?"

At that, he just shakes his head.

Right.

So *that's* how much he wants me to trust him.

One step forward, two steps back. I turn my back to him, but he puts his hands on my shoulders and spins me around to face him.

"What are you thinking?" he asks.

I look at him.

"I'm thinking that you need to take me back to America so I can decide, on my own, if I can ever forgive you or trust you."

At that, he shakes his head decisively. "No."

"No? Don't you want me to come to you on my own?"

"But you might not. So I'm keeping you."

"Well, if I didn't come back to you, wouldn't that mean we weren't meant to be?" My words are mean and spiteful, and I fling them at him anyway. I never used to be such a bitch. Not before I met Sergei.

"Don't say that to me!" His voice is a lion's roar, swelling up from deep within. I've hit him in a tender spot. His hands involuntarily bunch into fists. His eyes blaze with such rage that fear flares up inside me, and I flinch.

He points at the binders, and his words crack like thunder, ready to strike me down with their deadly force. "There are bookmarks on the table. Use them. Make three selections from each book. Now."

And he storms from the room.

I flip through the books, and I put paper markers between random pages in each one. It takes me two minutes.

I'm so angry with him that I ask him to let me sleep in another room that night, and he agrees with a mere nod.

I'm locked in the room at night. The door is opened for me in the morning.

We barely speak for the next few days. We eat meals together, but I parry away all his attempts at conversation, and he doesn't force it.

The closer to we get to the day he's scheduled for our wedding, the angrier I get. Exactly how stubborn is he? Would he really march me down the aisle by force on our wedding day? Doesn't he understand that would ruin any chance we have at happiness?

During the day, I read, I watch television, I sketch on an artist's pad that he has sent to my room. He spends most of his time in the office.

My mood has changed, and he knows it. I have to give him that. He doesn't force himself on me. He can sense when my "no" really does mean no.

When I see him, he's locked away in his own mind. He speaks in a formal, polite tone. He gives nothing away. I can't tell if he's angry, or sad. He moves through the day with brisk efficiency, acting as if our upcoming wedding is a business meeting that he's arranged and that I will definitely be attending.

Day ten...

I'm sitting in my room sketching a still life of a bowl of fruit when Sergei knocks on my door. The door is ajar, and I can see that it's him, but he still knocks.

I remember that terrible time when he first took me, when he and his servants burst into my room whenever they felt like it. When I dreaded every visit because I was being used as a weapon to hurt my uncle, which meant that I had to be hurt.

"Come in," I say, keeping my voice neutral.

He just stands there. "Darya is in the hospital. Here, in Pevlovagrad."

I scramble to my feet, panic clutching at me. "What happened?" I cry out.

His expression is grim as he leans in the doorway. "She came here to talk to Grigor, and she was hit by a car. Fortunately, it wasn't going too fast. Her injuries are minor."

I hurry towards him, and he steps aside. We head down the hallway together. "Was it an accident?"

"No. The men who hit her with their car got out and tried to drag her in, and the only reason she escaped is because she was carrying pepper spray, which slowed them down for a minute, and there happened to be a police car driving by. I think the only reason they didn't hit her harder was because they wanted her relatively uninjured."

"I need to see her! Get me my winter clothes, Sergei. Please."

He stops and puts his hand on my shoulder, and his voice is gentler and more patient than it has been in days. "I can't let you. It is too dangerous. This isn't me being a controlling asshole, although I am that. If you go there, even if I go with you and take a whole squadron of men, we're still at risk. And you're not just putting yourself in danger. You're putting her in danger, and every innocent bystander around us too. *Cataha's* looking for us, and he won't stop, and if he tracks us down there, innocent people will get caught in the crossfire."

Tears of frustration well up. "Damn it. She doesn't have any family. She needs a friend by her side. But I know I can't go. You're right. This just sucks."

He nods, sympathy glinting in his eyes. "I have four of my men at the hospital, guarding her. You can talk to her by

Skype. Come with me – I've got a laptop for you to use in the media room."

"Are you making any progress in catching him?" I ask, hurrying after him.

He glances back at me. "No. As cautious as he is being, it could take months. But it won't take forever. I'm doing the same thing he's doing. I've got a network of spies out there, I'm offering enormous amounts of money to anyone who gives up his whereabouts, and sooner or later he'll screw up."

I have to be content with that, for now.

In the media room, Sergei's security chief Andrei is standing by the desk, holding a laptop. He hands it to me, and I quickly settle down on a leather chair. Andrei and Sergei leave the room, a rare sign of trust from Sergei that thaws my anger at him a little bit.

Darya's waiting for me, with a rueful look. I'm relieved to see that she looks just fine; her face isn't bruised up at all. She tells me that the car hit her at waist level and knocked her over, and she has some bruising, but she'll be going home from the hospital that evening.

"Could Grigor have tipped the men off?" I ask her. "I hate to even think it, but..."

"No, you're right to be suspicious of everyone. I mean, I am too these days. It's a survival mechanism." Her blue eyes are an ocean of sadness and disillusionment. "But it couldn't be him, because I didn't tell him I was coming. I didn't tell anyone, I just took the bus. I was going to surprise him." She shakes her head. "I can't ever be with him. It would be too dangerous for him. It's just not meant to be."

"Bullshit."

She looks at me in shock. I don't swear often, unless I'm cursing out Sergei.

"Don't say that," I say heatedly. "Don't act as if you have no power over your own fate, because it's a terrible feeling and it's a vicious cycle. And you know what? It's lazy. It's an excuse. You think you're powerless, so you don't even try to change things. I did that for a long time when I was growing up, and I regret it. Obviously you care about him. I agree, given that he's right down the street from Club Hollywood, that it would be too dangerous to see him again in Pevlova-grad, but he could see you in St. Petersburg."

"You don't think some people are just born unlucky?" Her laugh is laced with bitterness. "Come on, Willow. My father died of a heart attack, my mother died of cancer. My older brother drank himself to death. I've been on my own since I was fourteen. And traffickers tried to kidnap me twice, and tried to run me over today."

No, I'm not letting her throw herself a pity party, because I know all too well how toxic it is to stew in your own misery. "You escaped traffickers twice, which few women do, and survived being hit by a car. You have me for a friend. Sergei put you in a great apartment in a beautiful city, and got you a fantastic job that you enjoy and that helps people. You're young, you're physically healthy, and you can make your own life into anything you want it to be. I'd call all of that lucky, wouldn't you?"

She manages a sad smile. "You're a good friend, Willow. I hope someday we can live in the same city. After *Cataha's* dead." She says that last bit with pure venom in her voice.

"Promise me you'll call Grigor and explain everything."

She narrows her eyes at me. "Aren't you a naggy-pants?"

"I'm the naggy-pants who isn't hanging up until you promise."

Her gaze drops. "What if I tell him and he wants nothing to do with me?"

"Then he's done you a favor by letting you know, and you're free to date someone else someday."

I hear raised voices in the hallway, and I could swear one of them is Slavik. He's back! And he's fighting with Sergei about something. Big surprise. Do these men ever have a peaceful moment?

"Darya, I'm going to let you go. If you promise to call Grigor! Do it!"

"I promise," she says, and I sign off.

I hurry to the doorway, and stop. The only way to find out what Sergei's really up to is to eavesdrop, because he still shuts me out of entire areas of his life.

"Sergei, you want my advice?" It *is* Slavik.

"Romance advice, from you?" Sergei barks out a harsh laugh. "The man who has, in his entire life, only ever had sex with prostitutes?"

"Hey, they have a lot of practice." Slavik's protest is good-natured. "So it's good sex."

"Thanks. I don't need your help."

"That's not what the servants are telling me. Yes, your butler has a big mouth. He says she's not even talking to you. You want her to trust you? Tell her the truth."

I suck in a gasp of outrage.

Sergei is still lying to me?

Sergei's voice is so sharp it could slice through diamonds. "I have told her the truth!"

"But you haven't told her everything."

"She knows I haven't told her everything."

"The thing that you're keeping from her...the truth about her parents...it's the thing that could set her free."

The truth about my parents? What could possibly be worse than knowing that my father was in his thirties when he married my fifteen-year-old mother, that he pimped out little children?

I storm into the room. I know that Sergei will be angry at me for eavesdropping, and I am beyond caring.

I can feel blood rushing to my face; I'm flushed with rage. My heart is hammering against my rib cage, and adrenaline burns through my veins. "What the *hell* are you supposed to tell me?" I shout.

"And there's your chance," Slavik tells Sergei. Slavik is still recovering from his beating. His head's been shaved, and I can see a healing line of stitches. His face is splattered with green and yellow bruises. He's leaning on a cane.

Sergei swings on Slavik. "What the fuck? You knew she was there!"

He doesn't even try to deny it. "Yes, I did. I saw her shadow."

Sergei's face flushes red, and he raises his fist. I fly forward, crying out, putting myself between him and Sergei. He accidentally strikes me on the side of the head, and I cry out and fall to my knees, pain pulsing in my right temple.

Instantly, he's on his knees by my side. "Oh God. Holy shit. Are you all right? I'm so sorry, Willow!"

My ears are ringing. "You punch like a bitch. I'll have to teach you how to hit," I mumble. It's something he said to me once, and hearing it, he manages a grim laugh.

Slavik is on his walkie-talkie. "I called for the doctor," he tells Sergei.

"I'll deal with you later," Sergei snaps. "Fucking asshole."

"Looking forward to it," Slavik says, and he strides off cheerfully, leaning on his cane.

Sergei helps me stand up and walks me to his bedroom.

Apparently, Sergei keeps a doctor on staff, because a white-coated man hurries through the door right after Sergei helps me to sit down on his bed.

After he examines me and makes sure I don't have a concussion, he surprises me by looking Sergei right in the eye and demanding, "Did you hit her?"

Sergei's eyes blaze with anger. "What did you just say to me?"

"Did you hit her? I won't tolerate that. I have daughters. I will not work for a man who hits women."

I'm overwhelmed with emotion. I've wanted so badly for just one damn person in the entire district to show that they have morals and a spine.

Before Sergei can say something horrible, I jump in. "He was trying to punch his friend, and frankly, that's the kind of thing these meatheads do all the time. Apparently it's what passes for social interaction with this group. It really was an accident."

"Well, all right then." He looks at me sidelong, then leaves.

"That was amazing," I say to Sergei. "It was worth it having you hit me just to have that happen."

His expression shows that he doesn't understand at all. "Have what happen?"

"To see that someone here can't be bribed or threatened. It's horrible, Sergei, how everything and everyone has a price. It makes me hate it here. It makes me want to hate humanity. It takes away all my faith. So to finally see someone brave enough to stand up for what's right here... that means a lot."

He looks disconcerted. "I don't want to see you hate people, Willow. That's not you. You always see the good in everyone."

"Not so much anymore." I settle back into the soft, puffy pillows and look up at him. He sits down next to me and reaches out and tries to touch my face, but I furiously swat his hand away.

I'm rigid with tension, and I grind my words out so there is no mistaking my seriousness. "What was Slavik talking about? What do you know about my parents? Tell me. I cannot stand living with secrets and lies anymore, Sergei." I punch him in the arm, hard. It doesn't hurt him, of course, but I want his full attention. "Tell me, or you will literally have to kill me to keep me here."

He looks as if he's about to argue, but then he catches the expression on my face. I'm not screwing around.

He takes a deep, long breath, and he's staring at me but seeing something else too. Looking into the past. It seems as if whatever he's about to say is so bad that he has to steel himself before he can speak.

Finally, he talks, and his gaze is full of pity.

"You're not a Toporov, Willow. Not really."

CHAPTER THIRTEEN

A wave of shock rolls over me.

My mouth opens and closes as I struggle to speak.

"Are you saying th-th-that I was adopted?" My voice cracks, and I have to push the words out.

He nods, a pained look stretching across his handsome features. "Something like that. Not legally. More like purchased."

His words are a bombshell hurled into my reality, exploding, shattering it. "That's crazy." I sit up, shaking my head in denial, my brown locks sliding into my face. Sergei reaches out to brush them back behind my ear, and this time I let him. "I mean...no. I look just like my mother. Everyone always said so."

"Yes. That's true. Your father chose you because you looked like your mother."

My father chose me. *Vasily Toporov chose me.*

I feel as if I'm slowly sinking into quicksand, but I force my mouth to move, to say things.

"Go on."

His gaze slides away from mine. "Your mother wanted a

baby. When it didn't happen, they did tests. It turned out your father was sterile. So you were adopted."

I struggle to reconcile that information. "If...if that's true...why didn't you just tell me sooner? I mean, plenty of people are adopted. I wish my mother had told me – but I understand why she might not have wanted to say anything. And it's not the end of the world."

He grimaces, looking really uncomfortable now. I've never seen this look on his face before. He's still not meeting my eyes.

There's more that he's not telling me, I can see. "What were the circumstances of my adoption?"

"That's the part I'd prefer not to discuss."

"Sergei!" I scream at him. "Damn it to hell, stop messing with me!"

His gaze snaps back to meet mine. "I'm not trying to!" he shouts back. "All right. Your birth mother was a prostitute."

I wince at that. "Okay. And my real father?"

"Unknown."

"All right." I feel light-headed. I'm turning this new version of my life over in my mind. "My mother wasn't my mother."

"But she loved you," Sergei rushes in. "I know that about her, because I spied on your family for almost a decade. There's very little about your family that I don't know, Willow. From everything I've heard, Tatiana loved you with her whole heart."

My heart hurts at the thought. My mother did love me. Well, the woman I called mother, anyway. She lived her life for me. She lived her life to make sure that I was the perfect little girl, to keep me safe from the wrath that burned just underneath my father's skin. We were going to go on the run together right after I graduated from college. We'd been planning it for years.

She would have risked my father's fury to save me from his terrible plans. She would have died for me.

"I don't judge my birth mother for being a prostitute," I say, struggling for breath. The thought of a woman so desperate that she had to sell her own child fills me with sorrow.

I can't sit still. I sit up straight, scattering the pillows, and swing my legs over the side of the bed.

"What choice do many of these women have, living in tiny, impoverished villages, with no job prospects?" I'm staring down at the floor while I say that, but I'm picturing women, their lips blue with cold, digging up grass to boil for soup. Crying children with distended bellies, curled up under thin blankets. "They can starve or sell themselves. I understand. She probably thought she was sending me off to a better life."

Sergei doesn't say anything, and the silence stretches between us like elastic, drawn too taut and ready to snap. I look up at him, and when he catches my gaze, he winces.

"What?" I demand.

He gives the slightest shake of his head. "Just this once, I wish that I could lie to you," he says. "Because the truth will hurt you. And it's not necessary. All you need to know is that you were given up for adoption and you had a mother who loved you more than her own life."

I feel tears shimmering in my eyes and I blink them away. Crying would be an insult to Tatiana Toporov, the woman who raised me and loved me. "Do you think I'm not strong enough for the truth?"

"I know you're stronger than anyone I've ever met."

I feel warmth fold through me. When he says things like

that, I believe him. His belief is the architect that builds me into a castle of stone.

"So tell me."

"When your father was on one of his business trips in Czechoslovakia, looking for little girls for his whorehouse, a woman approached him with a child for sale. You. You were one year old. You were a beautiful little girl, and you looked a lot like his wife, so he purchased you, but not to be raped. He gave you to his wife to raise as her own."

That hits me like a punch in the stomach.

I think I'm going to vomit.

Now I know why he hid the truth from me all this time.

Adoption I could handle. It stung, knowing that my family had kept it a secret from me my whole life, but I could spin the story in my head into a beautiful sacrifice by a loving, impoverished mother. Was already spinning it.

Now Sergei has torn the fragile web of lies apart with just a few words.

My real mother gave birth to me and then sold me off to be *raped*. When I was a baby. What kind of degraded fiend does that?

Am I crying? I think I am. I think I feel tears. I raise shaking hands to my face, but my cheeks are dry, my eyes are dry. I'm just shaking all over.

Sergei takes my hands and folds his hands over them. Normally when he does that, I feel as if I've been wrapped up in a blanket of infinite love and warmth. Right now, I'm numb. I can't even feel his touch.

An inner blizzard is forming, and I start to shake as it chills my soul. I don't understand what makes some people like that. Some people are born so dark, so evil, that it's truly as if they were spawned by the devil and sent to Earth to torment humans.

And my birth mother was one of those people.

Sergei sees the look on my face. "Willow, I'm sorry. I'm so sorry. I shouldn't have told you." He curses.

"No." I whisper the words. "You should have. You should have told me sooner."

He nods, a haunted look twisting his face. "Do you want to know her real name?" he asks gently.

That makes me shudder. "Not particularly. Maybe someday. Maybe never. She doesn't even feel real to me. She feels like a monster from a horror story."

Then it hits me. "Czechoslovakia? Lukas is Czech. And the second he saw me...it was like he recognized me."

"Yes. Lukas is your half brother. You look a lot like your birth mother, and that is why he thought you were her, returned for him."

Is he fucking *kidding* me?

Rage explodes inside me, and I slap his face so hard my hand stings. "Why didn't you tell me?" I scream. "I had a right to know! He's my brother, and you kept that from me? That is my family! What the fuck is the matter with you?"

"Because then I would have had to do what I just did!" Sergei cries out, and his eyes are twin mirror pools of despair. I've never seen him like this before. Not a hint of hardness, just devastating remorse. "I'd have had to take away your real mother and replace her with that pool of human sewage who would sell her own baby into sexual slavery. My own mother did the same thing to me and my brother, and to know that, it kills my soul and my faith in humanity. She sold us to be raped. She knew what would happen to us. I didn't want you to have a mother like that. It's poison. Knowing that the person who created you wants to destroy you...it's like a denial of your right to *exist*. I just... You deserve better than that."

He drops my hands, gets up and begins pacing. "I'm sorry. I am not saying I handled things well."

"No, you damn well didn't." I spit the words out bitterly. "And why do you even have him at all?"

He stares out the window as he answers me, shoving his hands in his pockets. "I went to Czechoslovakia to do some investigating. I was looking for any information that I could find on your family. I was constantly digging up pieces of their past to use against them. I found out who your real mother was, and I went to the village, and found out that she had..." he glances at me... "overdosed on heroin and died the month before."

I shudder.

Blow after blow.

My mother hated me.

My mother hated life.

"Her son was being cared for by the drunk next door, and..." He casts his glance down, and his gaze drifts far away. "He looked so much like Pyotr. So sweet and pure. His clothes stank of piss and he was starving, but he lit up with this huge smile when I walked in the door. So I took him away. Taking care of him...it was like taking care of Pyotr. Giving him all the things that Pyotr never had. Making sure that he was safe and fed and loved. Marya and Kris, I'm paying them, but they love him like their own grandson, and he truly believes they're his family, and he adores them." He's staring off into the distance now. "He has a magical life. A fairytale life."

And there are tears in his eyes.

He's in another world. Tears are brimming, threatening to spill, and his breathing is harsh, choked with sorrow.

The ice man is actually crying.

And all the hate drains from me as I think of the agony

that has chewed at Sergei's soul for so many years now. The guilt that he should never have to feel. A twelve-year-old boy blaming himself because his baby brother was raped by perverts. A boy who was ready to sacrifice himself to save his brother, but who accidentally survived instead.

My bones melt, too weak to hold me up. I sink back onto the bed.

Sergei is shaking as he settles in next to me, and tears spill down his cheeks, glittering in the lamplight. The long-buried agony is burning its way to the surface, finally released.

"I understand," I say gently, and I stroke his arm. "You saved Lukas from a life of starvation and abuse. You saved my little brother."

I don't want Sergei to hate himself, because he has no reason to. Sergei is his own worst enemy. Nobody can hurt him worse than his own mind.

Finally, Sergei tears himself away from wherever he went off to, and he looks at me, but he's got the thousand-yard stare of a man who's seen too much. "He can come live with us when we leave here," he tells me. "With Marya and Kris, of course – I wouldn't traumatize him by sending them away. We'll tell him that you are his sister, that he has a family."

I nod.

And then finally I start to cry. I'm crying at the lie that's been my entire life, at the joy and relief that I am in no way related to Vasily, at the sorrow of being hated so very much by the woman who carried me in her body for nine months.

I call up my mother, Tatiana Toporov, from the depths of memory. I force myself to picture my mother's face, which is not something I do often. It hurts too badly.

"I'm sorry." Sergei is hugging me tightly now, and I

need that. I need him so badly right now. "I'm sorry I told you."

"No." I sob into his shoulder. "Don't be sorry. I needed to know. You know...my mother is the woman who raised me. You haven't taken anything away from me. If anything, this makes me love her even more. I wasn't her flesh and blood, and yet she loved me so much. And I had seventeen beautiful years with her."

I'm curled up in a ball, and I cry and cry.

Sergei stays with me until finally I fall asleep.

When I wake up in the morning, he's still there, his arms wrapped around me, staring at me with love and tenderness. He actually slept in the same bed with me. The kiss that he presses onto my lips is as soft as clouds.

He strokes my hair out of my face and looks into my eyes.

"Do you love me?" he asks.

My heart swells in my chest. "Yes, I do."

"Will you marry me?" He's making himself so vulnerable asking that question. Sergei has metamorphosed before my eyes. He's letting me see a part of himself that nobody else sees.

But I close my eyes and remember the day he left me. The fear is still with me, the fear that a switch could flip inside him and I'll lose him again. He could turn back into the man who sat there calmly while I screamed and cried and broke in front of him.

His lies hurt me worse than the bullwhip that cut the skin of my back. Flesh can heal; the heart can only take so much before it's crushed beyond repair.

But can I imagine a life without him?

"I don't know," I tell him. "That's the best I can give you right now."

CHAPTER FOURTEEN

Day eleven, evening...
SERGEI

I am in my office working on designing security for a new building for Operation Salvat. The building houses former trafficking victims who have been freed and don't have homes to go to. Unfortunately, that's a lot of them. They became victims because they came from desperately poor situations and it made them take foolish risks. After they've been kidnapped, pimped out, drugged, forced to have sex with hundreds of men...they're released to face a whole new struggle.

They're traumatized, barely able to function, and either they have no families to go home to, or their families can't handle these damaged new versions of the women they once were. Mood swings, panic attacks, crying spells, too afraid to leave the house, unable to work...

So Operation Salvat, which I created and financed, offers them housing, education and counseling. We give them job training and get them employment, when they are ready. If they are going to testify against their abusers, we provide security.

When I had to tell Willow that I was a trafficker, it made me sick to my stomach. I wanted to turn around and run back to her, I wanted to scream that I had lied. I was pretending to be the thing that I loathed the most in the world.

Do I regret it?

I don't know.

It was a twisted situation. All the evil I'd done over the years, the people I'd killed, most of them deserving of it, but still...it poisoned my soul bit by bit until I was toxic and ugly and too foul for a pure, innocent soul like Willow.

Killing Vilyat and blowing up the trafficking ring had left a shocking void in my life, and I felt myself teetering over the brink. I could let myself fall, give in to pure evil. Chase after more and more power and money that I didn't need, kill rivals, kill their families, fight until finally I went too far and one of my enemies came for me in the night.

And it was tempting.

What stopped me from going that route?

Willow. If I turned into that kind of man, I would not be worthy of her.

And I couldn't just stay still. I had to change myself completely, one way or the other.

Willow pushed me towards the light, without even knowing it. Oh, I didn't fool myself into thinking that I could make myself into a sweet, soft man, nor did I want that. But striking a blow against evil felt like a step towards at least being able to move among humans and feel like one of them.

But I also knew without a doubt that coming back into the territory after I'd double-crossed high-ranking criminals and corrupt police alike was like running through a mine-field. And I knew my Willow. If I brought her here with me, she'd insist on getting down and dirty, on risking herself for women she'd never even met before. I couldn't keep her sitting behind a desk.

So I hurt the best woman I've ever known, and came here alone. It was like a punishment – like every other time I forced myself to stay away from Willow, but a million times worse. Like daily self-flagellation and then salting the wounds.

When she took her GPS tracker out, it was agony. I had my men following her, of course, but when she came to Russia she turned out to be damn good at hiding. Moving around, changing phones all the time, sleeping on people's couches. She didn't have an apartment; she lived out of her bag. She wasn't working; she had money because after I gave her the mansion in California and everything in it, she sold off a few hundred thousand dollars' worth of furnish-ings. She didn't buy a car; she took public transportation or rented cars. She went off the radar for a couple of months, but I knew that she was running around with that foolish group of anti-trafficking vigilantes, and I was sick with worry.

I was shocked and relieved when I figured out that she was regularly talking to Ludmilla and the journalists at *Reformat*. I snatched her up the first chance I got to take her back under my wing again.

And I realized that I wouldn't have lasted much longer without her.

I barely slept when she wasn't there. I moved through life in a burning rage. Food lost its taste for me. I worked eighteen, twenty hours a day, because when I wasn't work-ing, I couldn't stand to be in my own skin. The things that I was trying to accomplish – busting traffickers, setting up rescue networks for girls – they were getting harder and harder for me to do without her there.

Maybe if I put her to work doing something for Operation Salvat, it would keep her busy and make her feel like she was still helping. I don't want her to be bored, restless and miserable, but I also don't want to let her out of my sight, because I don't want her dead.

The door opens and Alexei bustles in, carrying a laptop. I feel that dull throb of sorrow that I didn't even know I was capable of when I think of Maks. Killing the last men on our lists made him worse, not better. Miserable, raging, spiraling out of control once we'd conquered our last demons. Driving alone like a fool after Slavik's brutal attack, when he should have been on high alert. Almost as if he was courting his own death.

The look on Alexei's face is grim, so I know the news won't be good.

"You've got a video call from *Cataha*," he says. "My men are trying to trace it."

He sets the laptop in front of me, and my vision clouds with rage.

Cataha, wearing his mask, is standing next to a man who's tied to a chair. It's Leonid, a member of my security team. Leonid's face is battered and bloody. *Cataha* is holding a knife.

"Sergei, you son of a pig," he says in his tortured rasp. Ha. He has *no* idea. I'm the son of *two* pigs, the unwanted litter from their disgusting rutting. "You have been causing me a lot of trouble. And you have something that belongs to me."

"I have a lot that belongs to you," I say. "Property, cars, money. And I will take even more. Including your life." I am sorry for Leonid, but this is the business, and if he let himself get taken, it means he was careless.

"Fuck you!" *Cataha* reaches over and viciously slices Leonid's ear off in one clean slice. Blood sprays out in a horrible red fountain, and Leonid's convulses in the chair before he screams and passes out.

"You're not a very good boss," he says reprovingly. "You've got a girl. She calls herself Natasha. Give her to me, and I will give you your man back. I mean if he doesn't bleed out first. And I will agree to a ceasefire if you stop trying to interfere with my operations. If you don't, more people will die, both yours and mine."

He wants Willow?

Cold, hard fury burns through me, but I don't let it show.

"Interesting," I say calmly. "I mean, you've got all the pussy you want – because you steal it, of course, the way a man does when he's so inadequate that no woman would be with him by choice. But nonetheless, you don't lack access to gash. So what's your interest in this particular piece of ass?"

There's the slightest chance that if I speak of her disparagingly, he won't realize her value to me.

"You stole her from me."

Now that's puzzling. Has he mistaken her for one of the girls we rescued?

"Bullshit," I snap at him. "She was never yours. And the only deal that I'll make with you is if you hand yourself over to me right now, I will make sure that your death is swift and far more merciful than you deserve."

Leonid's starting to come around. He's moaning and shaking with pain.

I do what I always do. Laser focus. Eyes on the end game. Let nothing distract me.

"Convince me," *Cataha* rasps. "Tell me her origin. Maybe I'm mistaken."

Like I'm a fucking moron. He'd never admit to making a mistake.

He's fishing for information for some reason that I don't understand, but I don't take orders from *Cataha*, or anyone. And I would never breathe a word of information about my Willow, not if it were to save my own life.

"Someday soon, you will regret that you didn't take my offer," I say.

"Today, your man will regret that you weren't more loyal," he says.

"He's already dead. And so are you, you piece of shit," I say.

Cataha turns his masked face to look at Leonid.

Leonid has finally accepted the inevitable. "Sorry, sir," he says to me, looking right at the camera. He *should* be sorry. He let this happen to him.

Leonid bites down on the poison capsule that my men carry in their back molars, and white foam spills from his mouth. His back arches in his death throes.

And I cut off the connection. It's the ultimate show of disrespect to *Cataha*, snatching his triumph from him.

I glance over at Alexei, who calls his man on his headset, but the news is bad. "Nothing, sir," he says to me with a frustrated shake of his head. So they weren't able to trace the video call.

If *Cataha* wants Willow, I've got to get her the hell out of here. Not just out of the district. Out of the country. There's too great a chance that someone will betray us.

I have the maids pack our bags for us quickly while I

make travel arrangements for us to head over to Sweden. I should reunite her with her brother anyway. I never had the right to keep her from him in the first place. I've wronged her in many ways, and I will spend the rest of my life making it up to her.

A few hours later, as we're sitting in the drawing room waiting for the maid to carry in our bags, I fill her in on what happened and ask her why *Cataha* thinks she belongs to him.

She's shocked, but then she tells me what he said to her back at the shopping center. Asking her name, where she was from.

A tsunami of rage sweeps me up in its whirling waters. *Cataha* dared to sully Willow with his filthy gaze. He probed her with his questions, tried to draw her into his web of perversion.

"Why in the hell didn't you tell me that?" I demand furiously.

"It didn't really seem to mean anything at the time." She shrugs weakly, looking bewildered. "I mean, it just seemed like questions from a crazy control freak. He didn't say anything about me belonging to him. He's got to have mistaken me for someone. He can't know who I actually am. I look nothing like I used to. My hair color, my hair style, all the makeup I wear these days..."

I run over possibilities in my head.

"Your father was going to marry you off after you graduated from college. You told me that once. Did he promise you to a specific person?" The mere question makes me blind with rage. The thought of anyone else marrying my Willow...

But she shakes her head. "No. I mean, he died a year before I even started college. He would probably have started looking for what he considered a good match for me a year before I graduated. Some gross old man who came from a connected family, most likely." Her face wrinkles in disgust at the thought.

"Here's the thing," I say. "I don't know why he wants you, or what he thinks he's going to get from you. But I do know that he has a reputation as a man who holds grudges, who is obsessed with revenge. If he thinks you're one of the women who escaped from him at some point, he'll come for you. And never stop."

"Would it help if we told him who I really am, then?" she asks helplessly.

I'm sick with anger at the thought of him knowing a single thing about her. It feels like he's trying to wrap his slimy tentacles around her and pull her away from me. "Absolutely not. Any information that we give him gives him power over us. And if he knows how important you are to me, it will make you even more enticing to him."

She shudders. "I get it. I really do, Sergei. I understand now why you lied to me."

When she says that, I feel a sudden lightness. The air tastes a little sweeter, and a tension I wasn't even aware of unknots inside me. I've spent so long beating myself up for all the things I've done to her, and for walking away from her, worst of all.

This feels like a step towards redemption. It feels like she might finally come to trust me someday.

Andrei pokes his head through the doorway. "The bags are in the car, and we're ready to go, sir," he says.

CHAPTER FIFTEEN

Day twelve, morning...
WILLOW

We are in a coastal city called Marslov, on the southwest shore of Sweden, and it's bright, clean and beautiful. I didn't realize how heavy the very air felt in Pevlovagrad until we arrived here. How it was never really light there, even in the middle of the day. How the grinding poverty and hopelessness suffused the bricks and mortar, seeped into the food until you could taste it with every bite. It saps the strength from people who live there, so that they shuffle and hunch as they move wearily throughout their long, gritty days.

Here, the air is clear and tastes like sunshine. People move happily and with purpose through the winding streets of a city built in the thirteen hundreds but still vibrant with life today.

It's obviously good for Lukas, who has grown like a weed since I last saw him eight months ago. We're at a beautiful house on a small, private island, which would be swimming distance to the city's shoreline if the water wasn't so cold, and Lukas is bouncing with joy this morning. Sunlight floods through floor-to-ceiling windows in the enormous family room with a spectacular view of the city. The furniture is light-colored wood, angular, classic Nordic design, with pillows and accessories in tones of blue and white. The floors are whitewashed wooden planks, the walls adorned with framed mirrors and sconces.

Sergei and I arrived at midnight and slept in a large bedroom on the second floor. The view from the bedroom window is indescribably beautiful, with the windswept bay and the city right beyond it, twinkling with a million lights at night.

Now we're joining Kris, Marya and Lukas for breakfast.

Lukas, wearing blue pajamas splashed with zoo animal pictures, crushes me in a surprisingly strong hug around the waist. I hug him back fiercely, a swell of emotion almost making me weep. *My brother. I have family.*

I'll tell him when the time is right.

"Willow! My friend Willow!" Lukas cries, bouncing on his bare feet. "I am going to be the ring bearer for the wedding!"

"Oh my goodness, really?" I say, sounding excited, but I shoot Sergei a dirty look.

"Yes, I will have a special suit," Lukas says happily. "Today they will measure me for it, and I will look very handsome. I am going to make you a wedding present that is a picture. Oh," he says, looking concerned. "Should it be a surprise?"

"No, it doesn't need to be a surprise," I assure him.

As we sit down to eat, I can't stop staring at him, trying to see our birth mother's face in his.

After a breakfast of fermented milk, muesli and fresh fruit, Lukas insists on taking me on a tour of the house, which has several wings and takes up a good part of the island. His artwork is everywhere, and it is amazingly good. An entire art studio is set up in a corner of his enormous bedroom. He favors colored pencils as a medium. He has a light, swirling touch, and everything he draws seems to glow from within.

He pouts and complains when Kris and Marya come to take him into town to get fitted for his suit, and makes me promise not to leave today.

Sergei re-emerges from the room he's using as an office there. He's wearing black slacks and loafers and a button-down white shirt. All his shirts must be custom tailored; that's the only way they'd fit his broad shoulders and massive biceps so well.

I am snug and comfortable in my blue yoga pants and T-shirt, but only because we're inside, toasty warm on this cold spring day.

He sits down with me on the sofa in the family room. He's settled into a pool of golden sunlight, lit like a Greek god. Even when he's casually sprawled on furniture, he's a lethal force. I can feel the tension coiling just under the surface; he's a lion sprawled on the branch of a tree, looking all loose and relaxed, but ready to pounce and devour.

A thrum of arousal warms my belly. The man is like walking Viagra for women.

"Word is, *Cataha* left the region for now," he informs me, his thick brows drawing together. "Headed northwest, in the direct of Moscow. But it could just be misdirection. I think the information came a little too easily."

I'm pricked by that little jolt of nausea and rage I feel every time I hear *Cataha*'s name. "Do you think Darya is safe?"

He nods. "It would be much harder for him to get to her

in St. Petersburg, and my men there are keeping an eye on her. Ludmilla's asking around, tapping all her sources, trying to figure out why he might be looking for you in particular. Who he thinks you are."

"Well, I guess that's all we can do right now." I lean back in my seat, casually sliding away from him. "Change of subject. Why did you tell Lukas that he's going to be the ring bearer at our wedding?" I demand.

His fierce grin holds a challenge. He's begging me to fight him on this. "Oh, don't you want him to be the ring bearer? He'll be so disappointed."

I glare at him. "I will agree not to try to leave your protection, or work with any anti-trafficking groups. At least until *Cataha's* dead. But I have not agreed that I will marry you. And there will be no wedding until I agree to it."

"How adorable that you think that."

He lunges and grabs me and pulls me onto his lap. He wraps his arms around me and pins me up against him. He's rock hard, and as I squirm and fight, I can practically feel his cock rising to meet me.

"Your name is Willow Volkov. You are the property of Sergei Volkov. I own your body, heart and mind. You are my wife in all but name, and in exactly eighteen days, in the drawing room of this house, with your family in attendance, it will be official."

I writhe in his grip. "No, it will not!"

His hot breath in my ear is sensual torment. "You're being a very bad girl."

"Sergei! I'm serious!" But it comes out as a moan.

"So am I. I am serious about marrying you. I am serious that I love you, and that I will do whatever it takes to protect you, even if you don't want me to. And I'll keep you with me until my dying day."

I try to be angry about his stalkerish claims on me. I try really hard. But with the feeling of his muscles bunching up as I try to fight my way out of his arms, it's difficult. "Do you understand how seriously sick that is?" My voice doesn't sound as stern as it should.

"Of course." He kisses my ear, and I stifle a whimper of pleasure. "By the way, I sent the kitchen staff away. Nobody here but my security team, and they're outside. We have the whole house to ourselves. And I told you what would happen if you tried to deny that you're mine." There's a low, rumbling threat in his voice.

I tense up, because I don't like the nasty gleam in his eyes. I try again to wriggle out of his arms, but he just tightens his grip until I feel like I'm being crushed by bands of steel.

"Sergei, please! You're hurting me!"

He growls in my ear. "Then sit perfectly still."

I obey him instantly – out of fear that he'll dislocate something on me if I don't.

"It's been too long since I've given you a real punishment."

I try to bargain. "We could...we could just have sex. It would be good. I love it when you fuck me."

Once he had to force me to say those words. Now they roll easily off my tongue.

"I know you do." He leans down and bites my shoulder, hard, and I cry out. "And I love to fuck you too. But I also love to punish you. I love it when you beg. And I told you what would happen every time you try to deny that you're mine. Didn't I?"

Despite myself, I'm falling into that quicksand of pleasure that will suck me in no matter how hard I fight. My body is turning soft and tender with desire for him.

"Yes, sir." It's the only answer I can give him.

He stands up, dragging me with him. Then, to my shock, he maneuvers me outside onto the deck, which faces the harbor. Immediately, I'm shivering as a cold wind whips off the water. The air reeks of seaweed and fish. I hear the hoarse creak of seagulls wheeling overhead. Boats are chugging by, crowded with bundled-up tourists, close enough that I can see people's faces.

I know what he's got in mind.

"No." There's anger, pleading and fear in that one word. Not in front of perfect strangers, in public. *No. I can't. I won't.*

I spin around to face him, and he slides one finger under my chin, tipping my face up to look at him. He's not shivering at all. He's not a normal man. Heat and cold don't touch him.

"You know how I love to give you choices, princess."

"Choices that aren't real choices," I protest.

He lets out a low chuckle. "Right now your choice is this. I'll fuck you out here, with no punishment, with you holding on to the rail as the boats go by. Or I'll take you inside and whip you twenty times with my belt and shove a butt plug up your ass."

"Not twenty times! Please!" I cry out, my eyes going wide with fright.

"I warned you. Decide now." He grabs the waistband of my pants. I'm shivering violently, from fear and anger and cold.

"Inside!" I cry out.

"I thought you'd say that."

He grabs me by the back of my neck and marches me into the house.

Our bedroom here – am I actually calling it our

bedroom? – has a huge four-poster bed, and he hustles me over to it. I stand there, shifting my weight from one foot to the other as he rummages in the nightstand and comes up with a rope, which he loops over the bedframe and uses to tie my hands.

Nervous anticipation curdles in my belly. He's leaving my shirt and pants on, and that's a good sign, isn't it?

The first smack of the belt across my back wrenches a cry from me, and shows me that thin fabric will not shield me from pain.

And then the second blow descends on me, and the third, and the fourth. I'm dancing in place, jerking against the rope.

I can hear Sergei's heavy breathing right behind me. It's arousal, not effort, that's making him breathe harder.

The smack across my butt cheeks makes me shriek. My cheeks quiver and a line of liquid fire runs diagonally across them.

"Stop it!" I plead. He ignores me and follows it up by laying several more stripes across my back. I can feel all of them, glowing as if coals have been rubbed on my skin.

He moves back to my butt, and I wriggle madly, trying to get away from him. I feel a steady throb of arousal between my legs, at war with the fiery pain splayed across my back.

"Please!" I cry out. "Stop it, now!"

Why are my nipples so hard? Why is my pussy so wet?

Crack. Crack.

"I choose neither!" My voice is raised to a shriek. "You can't make me chose between this and – owww! No! – this and being forced to – owww! No! Let me go!" I can barely catch my breath. "You're hurting me! Sergei, stop, stop, stop!" I scream, but he keeps cracking the belt across my agonized back and butt. Then he moves down to lash the backs of my thighs while I shriek and curse and sob.

He's painted liquid flame from my back down past my ass and onto my legs, and I'm panicked now, struggling wildly. I can't take any more.

I've lost track of how many times he's lashed me, and that makes me panic even more. My back is red agony, and I'm howling with pain.

When he finally lets me down, I collapse face down on the bed, legs hanging over the edge.

I cry into the comforter as he lowers my pants to my ankles. Pain travels down my back in steady waves. *Throb, throb, throb.*

He's opening up the nightstand and pulling out the butt plug.

"No more, no more! I'm sorry! I won't do it again!" I wail.

"Now, now, you want me to keep all my promises, don't you?" he croons as he drips icy-cold lube onto my puckered rectum. "I'm a changed man, Willow. You've changed me. Every word I say to you is true."

Then he presses his lubed-up fingers against it, and I sob harder, tensing up in a desperate fight to keep him from invading me. He won't be denied. He forces two fingers past my resisting ring of muscle, and he's inside me. I whimper in protest, but of course he ignores it. He spreads his two fingers apart, stretching my rear tunnel uncomfortably. "When I promise to do something, I've got to do it, so you see, I really have no choice in the matter."

My back and butt cheeks are still on fire, and now this?

"You don't have to punish me any more! The belt hurt, it really hurt!" I'm shaking with heaving sobs.

But he's merciless. He slides his fingers out and quickly

forces the butt plug inside me, stretching me out even more, and I groan in pain at the burning sensation that's blooming between my cheeks. He withdraws his hand, leaving the plug seated there.

Then he bends down and kisses the burning stripes on my butt, his lips soft and gentle.

"Of course it did. When I punish you, I don't fuck around." His fingers slide between my legs, and of course, I'm so wet that there's moisture dripping onto my thighs.

Then he moves, and his tongue is lapping up the moisture, and my sobs turn to groans of pleasure. "So sweet," he moans into my pussy. My whole body twitches as lightning bolts of pleasure zap down my nerve endings.

He slides his hand forward, massaging my clitoris, rubbing and rubbing. The comforter bunches in my hands as I clutch it. My breath is coming in pants now, and I spread my legs wide. My body has taken over my mind – it's opening for him and begging him to plunge in and destroy me.

The throbbing pain of the butt plug fades to a sweet ache. My back and ass are still on fire, but somehow, yet again, pain has melted into pleasure.

He stands up behind me, and when he pushes the thick head of his cock between my wet lips, I don't even pretend to fight.

"Yes," I hiss as he inches in bit by bit. He's stretching me to my limit, and my slick tunnel is clenching him tightly. "Oh...my...God, yes."

He slides halfway in, grabbing my hips and holding me firmly.

Then he stops, and I strangle on a scream of frustration.

"What's your name, baby?"

"Sergei, please!" I whine, and thrust myself backward –
but the bastard anticipates it and moves back away from me.

He chuckles as I whimper and squirm. "Pretty sure
that's not it." His voice is low and taunting.

Shamelessly, I wriggle, trying again to push back. To
make him push me all the way. A minute ago I was
screaming for mercy, and now I can barely stop myself from
screaming for more.

The low rumble of his laughter infuriates me. He loves
this most of all. He craves proof of how much I need him –
and to get it, he tortures me with desire until I'm completely
helpless. It's agonizing. I'd crawl over hot coals for him
right now.

Let me come. Please, please, please.

Just barely, I keep myself from shrieking the words out
loud. I won't give in so easily. He'll win in the end, but at
least I'll make him fight for it.

He moves ever so slowly, too slowly, sliding into me all
the way but without the force and friction that I need. Now
he's completely buried inside me and holding me perfectly
still. I kick my legs, I squirm my burning, punished bottom,
but I won't get what I need until I give him what he
demands.

"I can last all day," he intones, and I can hear the cruel
amusement lacing his voice. "What's your name,
sweetheart?"

There's only one way I'll get relief from the inferno of
need that's burning me from within. "Willow Volkov!" I
scream.

Fuck him, I don't have to mean it.

It's good enough for him, and he starts moving again,
thrusting hard, rewarding me for being a good girl.

He pumps in and out, and I hear his breath quickening.

It doesn't take more than a minute. I can't hold back any longer; I spill over the edge, the dam broken, pleasure cascading over me like hot lava. *Oh yes, oh yes, oh yes.* I hear screams of pleasure and realize they're my own.

Sergei is shouting my name, and his body is rocking into mine, and our pleasure twines together until we're one flesh and his orgasm is my own, and I'm falling into a white-hot netherworld that's made of agony and ecstasy.

CHAPTER SIXTEEN

Day thirteen...
WILLOW

After breakfast, Sergei retreats to his office and I go to the drawing room with Lukas, Kris and Marya.

Lukas is so excited about the upcoming wedding that he's making an entire picture book for us. It's supposed to be a secret, but he's terrible at keeping secrets.

And I'm really upset with Sergei for his attempt at manipulating me like this. Screw with *me*, fine, but does he have to drag my family into this mess? If he'd just be patient and let me make up my own mind, we wouldn't be having this problem.

But Sergei is never patient. He's a dormant volcano threatening to erupt at any moment.

"My friend Willow. Can you just sit there and look out the window and not move?" Lukas asks me. "Look, the bay is really pretty. You should just keep staring at it for a while."

It is beautiful, this city of wonders. It was built in medieval times. I stare across the bay at the gorgeous gothic church tower and the thirteen-hundreds architecture, the castle turrets at the south end of the city, the red brick town hall with the conical turrets like upside-down ice cream cones. I sit perfectly still and struggle not to let a smile twitch my lips as Lukas tries to sketch me in secret.

Kris and Marya sit and watch him, sipping coffee, with smiles wreathing their faces. I can feel how much they love him, and it warms my heart.

Sergei walks into the room a few minutes later. I can tell by his expression that something's happened.

"I can look out the window later," I assure Lukas. He looks disappointed, but lets Kris and Marya take him away.

A boat has pulled up to the island's dock, and as I watch from the window in the foyer, I see Slavik, Sergei's new security chief Alexei, and Ludmilla disembark. Ludmilla is limping, leaning on Alexei. Slavik is still using his cane.

"She was betrayed," Sergei says to me. "Someone revealed her identity. It's all over the internet now. She can't stay in Russia anymore; it's too dangerous. Not just *Cataha*, but all the corrupt politicians and cops, all the mobsters and traffickers she's exposed will be gunning for her."

Frustration boils inside me. I feel as if *Cataha* will never be caught, as if we're doomed to be on the run from him forever.

When Ludmilla makes it to the house, I see that her face is splotched with bruises, her lip split, her eyes blackened.

Alexei takes her luggage to a room in another wing of the house, and then she comes to join us in the drawing room.

"Do you need to go to a doctor?" I ask her, worried. "You look pretty beat up."

She settles gingerly onto the sofa. "I've already seen

one. I just need to rest and take it easy. I meant to apologize to you, Willow. I shouldn't have reacted the way I did when I found out your identity. Of course it's not your fault that your father did what he did."

I don't bother to correct her that Vasily isn't my father, but I do feel happier just knowing it. Lighter, freer. I haven't had any of my attacks since Sergei told me, haven't been tempted to claw at my own flesh.

It has been an enormous weight off my conscience. It shouldn't make such a difference, but somehow it does.

"Think nothing of it. I'm just glad you're all right. How did you get away from them?" I ask her.

"Pepper spray. And there were some people nearby. These men attacked me as I was walking to my car in a grocery store parking lot. I screamed a lot and sprayed them, and they ran away." She shakes her head sadly. "It's the end for me, I'm afraid. Akim is no more."

The thought of letting *Cataha* win so easily infuriates me.

"But you can't let Akim die," I protest. "*Reforma* can keep putting out stories and say they're from Akim."

"No!" Ludmilla protested instantly. "That puts everyone at *Reforma* at risk."

I'm getting madder and madder. Why is she just rolling over? Yes, it's very frightening. That comes with the territory, and she knew it when she took the job. It's just not right, letting *Cataha* win like this.

Sergei, thankfully, agrees with me. He makes a gesture of impatience. "I created Akim, not you," he says to her, his voice rough with anger. "You can check the contracts that you signed with my lawyers if you disagree. I decide what Akim does. Akim is not a person – he or she is a symbol of resistance and change. And as for the people at *Reforma*, they can choose whether or not to continue publishing Akim's stories. If they don't, Akim and all my financing will move elsewhere."

Wonder and respect bloom inside me. I had no idea that he was the creator of Akim.

"You're right. You're right. I'm sorry, Sergei, I've just seen too many pictures of *Cataha*'s victims. I don't ever want to see that happen to my co-workers at *Reforma*." Her voice is hoarse with sorrow. "That look on their faces. How long it takes them to die..." Tears spill onto her bruised cheeks.

"That's their choice, though," Sergei says to her.

I feel a brief flash of resentment. How nice that he lets them make choices. I wish he'd extend the same courtesy to me.

Ludmilla just nods wearily. "I'm going to go lie down for a while."

"How did you create Akim?" I ask him after she limps away.

"I recruited Ludmilla to write the stories under the pseudonym of Akim, because she was an excellent journalist and I knew her past, how she'd lost her sister and never stopped looking for her. I convinced *Reforma* to hire her. I paid *Reforma* millions of dollars for security and to pay the salaries of their reporters, and took them from a tiny little newspaper to a massive worldwide presence that's impossible to ignore." He shrugs. "But I won't accept credit when I don't deserve it. It sounds heroic and noble, but it wasn't. That was all part of my long game. To bring down the men on my list."

"Are you sure?" I ask him. "There were lots of ways you could have taken them down. You could have kidnapped them and tortured them for days, weeks, months. But you did it in a way that cost you a lot more money, took a lot more time, and struck a massive blow to the flesh trade. I think you don't give yourself enough credit. You do too many good things for people to have it just be an accident."

He chews his lip thoughtfully and frowns, but for once he doesn't argue with me.

Since he's not in one of his combative moods, I try to press my advantage. "Can we please talk about the wedding? I'm asking nicely, Sergei."

He stands up, and I think he's about to give me grief, but instead he shocks me. "We're going to go on a date this afternoon."

"What?"

He sighs. "Let me rephrase that. May I take you out on a date this afternoon?"

He's actually *asking* me? Sergei Volkov is giving me a real, genuine choice?

"You really want to take me out on a regular date, like normal human couples do?"

"Yes." He nods vigorously. He looks so serious, so hopeful even, that I couldn't possibly consider saying no. "When we're married and it's date night...what would that look like?" he says.

I consider that. "Well, so far you've always made all the decisions. So let's say we'd take turns with that. Sometimes I would pick what we do. I'd want to go for a walk by the waterfront, and then to an art gallery, and then dinner at a restaurant of my choice. And...I'd want to choose my outfit."

He stands up. "Let's do this! You tell me the restaurant, I'll make the reservations. I do need to run it by my security team, but there shouldn't be any problems."

I glance at him, suddenly feeling shy. After all my

protesting about wanting to make my own decisions, I'm about to make a silly request.

"Sergei?"

"Yes?"

"I know I'm choosing everything else but, but...I want you pick my outfit. I kind of like it when you do that. I don't know how, but...you always pick the perfect outfit for me. It's like you know me better than I know myself sometimes."

When Sergei dresses me, I feel as if he's with me all the time, in a way, wrapping me in his strength like a cloak.

"Yes, it is, isn't it?" He tips my head back and kisses me softly. "Yes, Mrs. Volkov, I will pick out your outfit for you this afternoon."

SERGEI

I'd love to lie. I'd love to say this feels natural, but it doesn't. I feel like a tiger that's been let loose in a crowd of gazelles, whipping its head around, deciding where to sink its fangs in first.

I want to bark orders at Willow. I want to tell her to do impossible things, just to force her to resist. I want to see Willow fight me. I want to see the look in her eyes when she realizes she's lost yet again. The humiliation, the submission, the angry acceptance. Then the craving. The raw hunger that I've forced on her.

And sometimes she wants that too, but not all the time. It can't be like that all the time, or I'll lose her. I want her caged, yes, but I want her to stride right into that cage happily. If she's truly miserable, then by winning, I've lost.

This is much harder than I thought it would be.

Before I met Willow, my entire life, every human interaction was a fight, a negotiation, a brutal establishment of my dominance.

I always moved and spoke and acted in a way that let others know that my word was law and defiance was death. I didn't make dates. I made battle plans.

But today I will force myself to be what Willow needs, for once.

I have dressed her warmly, in black wool slacks, a sparkly black sweater, black puffy down coat, and fur boots. I'm wearing my heavy leather coat and a hat, which probably isn't even necessary. The cold doesn't seem to touch me. Maybe it doesn't dare. Maybe like recognizes like.

My guards trail discreetly behind us.

We wander through a historic district, towards a bridge that leads to the restaurant she's chosen, our breath puffing in the frosty air.

The wind catches the strands of Willow's hair and whips it into her face. I stroke it out of the way. She still has her hair extensions in, and I know she still keeps little blades and lock picks hidden in them. I haven't taken them from her, because I want to let her have at least the illusion of freedom.

And I can't deny, I like that side of her. There's a part of her that's weird and crazy and feral just like I am, and it calls to me, sings to me, tells me that she's my perfect match. The yin to my yang.

We keep walking, in silence.

Normally my silence is strategic. Make my enemies wait, anticipate, fear what I'm about to say. Now I'm just walking down the street with my fiancée, staring at the sights as if I've never seen a city before. In a way, I haven't. Not like this.

The architecture in this historic walking distance is a

mix of styles, from the twelve hundreds to the sixteen hundreds. Aesthetically, it's stunning. The cobblestone streets are narrow, and tourists are goggle-eyed with awe, gathering in clots to snap picture after picture.

Distracted. A herd of baaing sheep. If an assassin wanted to take them out, they'd never see it coming.

I start idly performing a threat assessment. Looking for areas that might conceal a sniper. The rooftops would be ideal; you could run from rooftop to rooftop for blocks on end. Doorways are less than optimal. Yes, they're deepset and plunged in shadow, but the street is crowded and there are no vehicles here, so it would be difficult to escape after – *no. I'm not doing this, not today.*

I look at an older couple who are holding hands. They're staring at a church built in the fourteen hundreds, in the Danish brick gothic style. He's telling his wife that they used bricks in those days because the areas around the Baltic sea didn't have natural stone resources. I'm thinking about how easily the stained-glass windows would shatter under a hail of gunfire.

Willow reaches out and grabs my hand. I stiffen, then force myself to relax and squeeze her hand in mine. I hold her hand, but I am aware of it with every single footstep.

It feels unnatural. She's grabbing my right hand, which limits my ability to grab the Glock tucked into the holster on the left side of my waistband. In the event of an attack, ripping my hand from hers would cost me as much as three crucial seconds if I needed to go for the pistol.

And more than that – it makes me feel naked and vulnerable in a way I haven't experienced since I was a little boy.

Forced to display my feelings to the world. My soft, girlish feelings.

This is the part where, once upon a time, I'd have torn away from her and said something cruel. Or where I'd have dragged her into an alley and bent her over a garbage can, or forced her to her knees and made her service me while she cried in fear that someone would see us.

But not today.

It didn't even occur to me to hold her hand; she had to initiate it.

Sweat beads on my forehead.

How do you walk down the street with your fiancée? *How is it done?*

I look around us now and observe how other couples walk. Normal couples. Hands around each other's waists, gazing into each other's eyes. They make it look natural. They move in rhythm with each other, pausing at the same time, turning their heads towards each other as if directed by some unseen voice.

It's like there's this whole world out there that I've never let myself see. I've lived in an alternative universe that was always a war zone. I've scanned the world through the eyes of a despotic king. I've evaluated strengths and weaknesses, probed for hiding spots and ambushes.

Willow looks around and sees beauty and kindness and love.

Can I really do this?

Can I give my Willow the life she deserves?

The answer is, there is no choice. I can't live without her. Not if I want to stay sane.

I crave her sweetness, her laughter, her humor, her kindness. I crave her approval. I want her to look at me with that light of admiration shining from her eyes. I want to be worthy of that look she gives me.

"Thank you," she says suddenly, stopping. And I realize

that my tensely drawn muscles have started to relax, and I've walked the entire length of the street and onto the bridge, holding her hand. She slips her hand out of mine and she circles my waist with her arms, but stands there, tentative, unsure.

"The pleasure was all yours," I tease her, and pull her up against me for a long, hungry kiss.

She laughs happily. "You jerk."

"How observant of you. I'm also the jerk you're going to marry in seventeen days."

She looks as if she's about to argue, then bites her lip.

"That's right," I tell her, tipping her head up and forcing her to look into my eyes. "The rules still apply. If you defy me, you think I won't take you right here on the bridge?"

"What if we got arrested for indecent exposure?"

"I have very good lawyers on retainer."

"Fine," she says, her gaze dropping submissively. "This is me not arguing. This is me not saying a word."

This little battle of wills, which I've just won, makes me so hard. And I realize I don't need to break her into pieces in order to get my rocks off. This is more than enough for me.

She's taking deeper breaths now, and I can tell that she's turned on too. She loves my dominance. I don't always have to lace it with brutality.

And as we walk to the restaurant, hand in hand again, I'm smiling. I think I can do this. We're a match. She needs me as much as I need her. Her light needs my darkness.

The maître d' sends the waiter off to see if our table is ready.

She's happier and more relaxed than I've seen her in ages. The smells of butter and garlic and sizzling meat drift our way, and she inhales deeply, drawing them in.

"Will you sleep in bed with me again tonight?" she asks, her voice soft and hopeful. "With me in your arms?"

"I will. By the way, I could see that you were about to argue with me about the wedding. But since you were such a good little girl and you stopped yourself, I'll wait until we get home before I punish you."

"Now I get punished when you just *think* I'm going to argue with you?" Her voice rises in an indignant squeak. Then she blushes and glances quickly at the maître d' to make sure he didn't hear her.

I slide my hand under her coat and squeeze her ass cheek, hard enough to hurt her a little, and she lets out a whimper.

"Yes. Do you have a problem with that?"

"No," she says, trying to squirm out of my grip, but I grab her arm and hold her still.

"How about 'sir'?" I say to her, smiling gently. "I like it when you say sir."

"Yes, sir," she murmurs. "I don't have a problem with it."

Now all I can think about is rushing her through dinner so I can get her back home.

CHAPTER SEVENTEEN

Day fourteen...

Sergei waits until after breakfast to drop the next bombshell on me.

"Perhaps Ludmilla would like to go with you to your wedding dress fitting today," Sergei says to me, and his eyes have gone winter cold again. "You're to be there in an hour."

This is the first I've heard of it. Anger prickles underneath my skin.

Sixteen more days.

Every time I start to relax and just try to enjoy getting to know this newer, kinder version of Sergei, he has to throw this in my face again. I feel as if a golden noose is tightening around my neck and strangling me. Yesterday he was funny, sweet, sexy Sergei. Now he's got that angry, challenging look back on his face, daring me to say a single word about my own fate, my future.

"Oh, that's today? Sure, I would love to go," Ludmilla says, looking surprised.

"But Sergei, she can barely walk. We should postpone it," I protest.

He gives me a look, but I don't drop my gaze. I know that last night's date was an attempt at distraction. And it was a wonderful, perfect night, right down to the rough sex we had when we got home. But that was *one night*.

"We can't," he says with a hint of danger in his voice. "This was a rush job already."

I want to scream, *And whose fault is that?* But I don't dare.

Maybe if Sergei had been raised like normal people, he'd understand me. He thinks he can control everything and everyone around him. All he has to do is bark out an order, and he gets it. Every time.

What he doesn't comprehend is that while you can control people's actions with brute force, you can't control feelings.

And no matter how hard I try to tell him, he won't listen.

"I am feeling much better," Ludmilla assures me. "I really would like to get out of the house, and this sounds like so much fun! It'll get my mind off things."

Great. So if I say no, not only do I get in trouble with Sergei, but I'm the jerk who's making Ludmilla sit around stewing in misery.

"I'll go get on some warmer clothes," I say.

"I've got them lying out on the bed already," Sergei informs me.

Not today.

When I walk into the room, I spare one quick glance at the clothing he's laid out on the bed for me. A rose-colored cowl-neck sweater, black velvet slacks. Beautiful. Normally I'd love to pull that sweater over my head, knowing that he picked it out because he thought it would be perfect for me. Today, if I wore it, I'd feel as if it were strangling me.

I deliberately go into the closet – which at least isn't locked, thank God for small favors – and pick a different outfit. A long, plum-colored wool skirt, thick winter tights, a mauve turtleneck sweater. And I take my time about it. Sergei's brows draw together in a scowl when he sees what I'm wearing, but I ignore it.

We take the boat across the water in uncomfortable silence, just me and Ludmilla and Sergei and ten body-guards. *Ten.* How long will our life be like this?

Ludmilla glances from Sergei to me and back again. She can obviously tell that something is wrong, but wisely, she doesn't ask.

There are cars waiting for us at the boat dock. The bridal shop is a short trip into town, one in a row of shops on a cobblestone street. The drivers pull over to let us all pile out, and I can't help but think how ridiculous we must all look.

"I'll wait outside," Sergei says. "Bad luck for the groom to see the bride in her dress before the wedding."

We pause outside the shop, and as Ludmilla heads into the store, I draw Sergei aside.

"I am officially, seriously pissed off at you right now," I snap at him. "You're taking what could be a joyous occasion and making it miserable for me by not letting me have any choice in it. I am going to go in there and put on a happy face for today, but if you don't at least postpone the wedding, I am going to stand right up there on our wedding day and tell everyone that I will not marry you. And I don't care if you beat me black and blue when we go home. I don't care if you beat me until I pass out."

Nobody speaks to Sergei like that.

Rage and shock bloom on his face, but I don't wait for a reply. I just hurry into the shop.

I have to pause and take an enormous gulp of air and let it out again to keep from screaming in fury.

Tension and misery are making me queasy on the day when I'm getting fitted for my wedding dress. I refuse to feel guilty about being such a bitch. I have every right.

I stand stock still for a moment, trying to brace myself. There are mannequins draped in gorgeous gowns everywhere, and I feel like they're mocking me with the smiles on their plastic lips.

Two attendants are eagerly hurrying towards me, and there are no other customers in the store. Sergei probably booked the whole morning just for me. I swallow a lump in my throat.

A million emotions are swirling through me right now. *I miss my mother so much. I don't have a father to walk me down the aisle; I've got nothing but the memory of a monster. This isn't how my dress fitting is supposed to feel. My fiancé and I are fighting, and for that matter is he even my fiancé? He never officially asked me. I want to cry. But I won't cry.*

I feel so alone.

I look for Ludmilla, and see her at the other end of the shop, pacing and talking on her cell phone.

I reach up and pat my hair, sliding my finger between the strands. My lock picks, my handcuff key, they're all there. I take them out every night and clip them back in every morning after I shower.

I glance at the shop window and see Sergei standing there with his back to the store, rigid with anger. This isn't what I wanted. I just want time. I just want him to understand me. I just want him to let me have a little bit of control over the most important decision in my life.

I feel a sudden urge to run out there and tell him that I love him, plead with him not to be angry with me. I hate it when he's genuinely angry with me. I need him. I want him. Why can't he just work with me a little?

But I've said those words to him so many times that even I'm sick of hearing them. My words have lost all power – they just hit Sergei's force field of rage and tight control and slide right off.

I feel weary and defeated as I let the shop attendant lead me down the hallway, and I can't help but notice that there's a door open at the end of the hallway – leading to an alleyway behind the shop.

I could run.

But I said I wouldn't.

Why do I have to keep my promise to a liar?

I go into the fitting room, change into the dress, and just stand there as if I'm in a dream. I'm floating off in space somewhere while the attendant and her assistant fuss over me with measuring tapes and dress pins. They try to make conversation, but I'm mumbling answers, staring at the wall.

The dress is a sleeveless ballgown style with a lace illusion neckline. It's stunning, it's perfect for me, and it makes me want to weep. And not with joy.

Ludmilla comes in a few minutes later and joins me in the fitting room.

"Everything all right back home?" I ask her.

She smiles wearily, glancing at the attendants, who are on the other side of the room, chattering to each other in Swedish. "Yes," she says in a low voice, speaking in Russian. "They're picking a new reporter to be Akim. It's all right. It was a good run. And you look beautiful, by the way."

I glance at myself in the full-length mirror. Can she not see the pinched, unhappy look on my face? Is it just me?

Minutes tick by as they take my measurements, and

then I'm changed back to my regular clothes and looking at trays and trays of veils and tiaras.

Ludmilla's phone rings, and she rolls her eyes. "Crap. I forgot to turn off the ringer. Let me just take this one call and I'll turn it off."

She hurries out of the room.

A minute later, she sticks her head in the door and waves at me frantically.

I hurry out into the hallway. Her eyes are wide with horror.

"He's got Darya," she whispers.

I don't need to ask who. She shows me the screen on her phone, and I see a picture from my nightmares. Darya's angry, tear-stained face, staring right at the camera. There's a gun barrel pressed to the side of her head.

She has a black eye and a split lip.

A wave of panic swells up and threatens to drown me. I lean against the wall, and my throat closes tightly. I can't even imagine what she's feeling right now. *No, no, no.*

"We need to get her back. What does he want? Did he say?" I demand. I glance at the two attendants in the fitting room. They're ignoring us right now, taking notes and chatting with their backs to me.

"He sent me a message saying that he would trade her for you." Ludmilla avoids my gaze. "It's your choice. To be honest with you, I probably wouldn't do it."

Brave Ludmilla, who's risked the wrath of the traffickers for years? She would. And so will I. "Don't sell yourself short. Here's what we do. We can make this work. We're going out the back door. Send him a message. Tell him that we will meet in Pevlovagrad at the Brick Market in six hours, and he needs to let her get out of the car and I need to see her walk away to safety before I'll hand myself over.

We'll meet over by that stall that sells all the Soviet memorabilia."

"And then what?" she protests.

"If we rush to the airport right now, Sergei won't realize we're gone before it's too late. Right as I'm about to get on the plane, I'll send him a message telling him what I'm doing, so he won't be able to catch me, but he'll be right behind us. I have a GPS tracker implanted in my right leg. If *Cataha* takes me...it will lead Sergei straight to him."

Her eyes widen in surprise. "My God. This might actually work." Then she looks at me searchingly. "It's a huge risk, though, you know that."

"Yes, I know that. It's a worthwhile risk."

I don't even want to picture Sergei's rage – or his hurt. I've got to get out of here before I change my mind, because I'm utterly terrified. What will *Cataha* do to me before Sergei comes for me? What if Sergei can't find me?

But I have to do this. This is my chance. It's not just rescuing Darya – it's ending the reign of terror in the Pevlova Oblast.

We hurry down the hallway and out the back door before anyone notices that we're missing. I'm surprised that Sergei doesn't have a man stationed there just in case. Or is that just me being paranoid? How far is *Cataha*'s reach? Has danger followed us here to Sweden?

We're rushing through the alley when the wind suddenly shifts and I smell the coppery scent of blood.

A lot of it.

I spin around. "Something's wrong."

Ludmilla grabs my arm and tries to pull me.

"We've got to hurry!"

"I smell blood!"

Her voice goes high and shrill. "Are you crazy? You

don't care about Darya at all, do you? She's probably being raped right now – you've got to save her!"

But I wrench my arm from her grasp and hurry back down the alleyway, and then I see it. A pool of blood, spreading out from behind a cluster of garbage cans.

I lean over the cans to look, and a thunderbolt of shock strikes me so hard I stagger. Two of Sergei's men, face down, knees to their chests, stuffed back there hastily to hide them. Dead.

Ludmilla. The weird way she's suddenly acting.

How *did* she get away from *Cataha*'s man when they beat her up? Answer: she didn't have to. The attack was a fake. Staged. So that she could beg Sergei to take her in.

That phone call she was making in the dress shop...she was calling *Cataha*. She'd probably already told him where we were, so he had his men standing by in the city, just waiting for their chance.

I spin around to face Ludmilla, whose face is so hideously twisted with rage that I don't even recognize her, and draw in my breath to scream.

She is holding a syringe, and she jams it into my shoulder through my coat so fast I don't even have time to struggle. It's like being stabbed with a red-hot knitting needle. The wind swallows my cries and the world goes all wavery.

The last words I hear are, "Fucking Toporov *bitch*. That's for my sister!"

CHAPTER EIGHTEEN

What day is it? How long have I been out?

The first thing I feel is cold. Bone-chilling cold radiating up from the ground, sucking the heat and life from my body.

The next thing I feel is pain. Throbbing pain in my right leg.

"Willow. Willow. Are you awake?"

I sit bolt upright, strangling on a scream of fear.

There's a nasty chemical smell in the air. It stings my nose and makes me feel queasy.

Where they hell are we?

I fling my hands out, and they strike something cold and metal. It's dark in here; I can barely see. But by feeling around, I realize that I'm in a cage. Like an animal. It's not quite tall enough for me to stand up in.

I'm in a cage.

The realization fills me with horror.

Struggling not to scream, I squint in the darkness, looking around the room, and finally I see Darya, in a cage next to mine. She's curled up on a thin mattress, hugging her knees, with a blanket wrapped around her. Barefoot, wearing leggings.

I can't make out much in the darkness, but I see a chair that looks as if it's bolted to the ground, and a chain hanging from the ceiling.

I scrabble around in my cage and see that I have a mattress and blanket too, so I crawl up on the mattress and wrap the blanket around me. It's thin and scratchy, but it helps repel the chill a little bit. I'm only wearing leggings and a long-sleeved shirt.

I don't feel an ache between my legs, so I'm pretty sure I haven't been raped. Yet. But this kidnapping is entirely different from the fake one that Sergei staged. He made sure that I woke up in a warm, clean room with water sitting nearby.

Whoever has taken us wants to make sure that Darya and I are humiliated, miserable, and physically weakened.

Sergei will come save us. Sergei will come save us. I chant in my head, a desperate mantra, a tiny spark of hope to cling to. *How long have I been here? Why isn't he here yet?*

I suck in breaths of cold air, and gradually the dizziness fades. My eyes adjust to the darkness. We are alone in the room.

I'm horrified to see that there's a bucket in the corner of the cage. Darya has one too, and now I can smell urine wafting in the air.

They want to reduce us to animals.

"Darya? Are you all right?" I mumble, then realize what a stupid question that is.

"Not really." She makes a sound that could be a sob or a laugh.

"You called me Willow. How did you know my real name?"

"They told me when they brought me here. They said I was just bait for you. Willow, you shouldn't have come for me," Darya groans. "Why did you do it?"

"I had a plan," I croak, and realize I am desperately thirsty. "This wasn't part of it. How did they get you?"

She shifts on the mattress, wrapping the blanket around her more tightly. "I'm so stupid. That bitch Ludmilla... We were both at work, and she asked me if I wanted to go out and grab a drink after work. I said yes. I honestly thought it was weird – she's never been warm and friendly in the couple of weeks I've known her; she was always just pure business. But I was lonely and wanted a friend, and I felt kind of intimidated by her because she's such a big deal at *Reforma*. So I went anyway. And of course...she drugged my drink. Can you fucking believe it? I mean, I would say I'm never going to go out for a drink again, but that's not an issue. Because we're both going to die here." Her voice rises in a hysterical laugh.

I want to reassure her, but how can I?

I have to admit to myself – even if Sergei gets to us in time, I'm sure the place is heavily guarded. We'll probably be murdered before he can rescue us – and that's the best I can hope for. That our suffering will be over quickly.

And all this at the hands of a woman I admired so much. A woman I trusted with my life, many times.

"I can't believe she did that to you. I can't believe I was so wrong about her," I groan. "Of all the people to sell out for money. How could she?"

Darya coughs, and her body shakes. "It wasn't money. She told me that *Cataha* promised to return her sister to her. Sabina. Her sister was taken eight years ago, and she'd given her up for dead, but *Cataha* showed her a recent picture of Sabina, holding up a newspaper from just a week ago. And she said that your family were the ones who took her sister in the first place. Is that true?"

"Yes, it was my father." *I am hurtling off a cliff. Falling and falling.* "But she shouldn't have taken it out on you. What happened?"

"She told me she was sorry that she'd had to involve me, but there was nothing she wouldn't do to save her sister. And she said you deserved it. I don't believe that, though. You didn't know, did you?"

"Oh God, no."

I can't just sit here like this. I have to take action or I'll go crazy. I crawl over to the cage door and test it. It's locked, of course. I reach up to my hair, then suddenly realize that my head feels strangely light.

All my hair extensions have been cut off. Frantically, I run my fingers through my hair, but every single tool that I had is gone.

Then I realize why I have an ache in my right leg.

The true horror of my situation hits me.

Sergei will never find me. I'm going to die here.

Because I told Ludmilla about the tracker, which means they would have searched my body for it and found it. The tracker would have been removed before they brought me to this hell pit.

Everything is gone. My blades, my lock pick, cyanide pill.

And even worse, I wonder – will Sergei think I ran, on purpose? Will he suspect me of murdering his men so I could escape? Is that a crazy thing to worry about? I don't know. I'm so dazed with fear and thirst and terror that I can't think straight.

Tears fill my eyes and spill down my cheeks. I always knew that it would come to this, but it's no less terrible.

I'm twenty-three. I don't want to die. I want to see my family again. I want to see Sergei again. I don't want him to hate me. I don't want him to think I ran away from him after I promised not to.

I want water. I'm so thirsty.

"I called up Grigor like you said, and he was going to meet me in St. Petersburg." Darya's voice is a pained croak in the darkness. "He'll think I stood him up. *Reforma* will think that I just quit without notice. Ludmilla will make them think that, because she's their shining star. Their heroine. You still think Fate doesn't hate me, Willow?"

I can't even find words to answer her. I just hug myself and rock silently.

Time ticks by, too slowly. Minutes? An hour?

Finally, I force myself to form words.

"We fight to the end, Darya," I rasp.

"Yes." She clears her throat, which I'm sure is as dry as mine. "You were my friend. Thank you for being my friend."

And then the door flies open, and I choke in fear, because the devil is striding through.

He's still wearing his mask.

They flip on the lights and flood the room with blinding white light. Tears burn in my eyes, and I blink frantically.

He has four men with him. Without a word, they open up Darya's cage. She scrabbles to the back of the cage, and one of the men pokes a cattle prod through the bars, making her scream.

I want to cry out in protest, but what's the point? These men thrive on inflicting pain and fear.

She crawls out of the cage without a word, and tries to

stand up, but one of the men kicks her back down to the ground, grabs her by the wrist, and drags her across the floor.

Because she's not even human to them. They have to degrade her in every possible way. She would have walked, but they want her knocked down and helpless.

When they reach the chain dangling from the middle of the room, they tear her clothes off. My stomach turns to water.

They'll rape her while I watch.

They tie her hands to the chain that's dangling from the ceiling. Then one of the men turns a crank on the wall so the chain is pulled up, and she's hauled up off her feet. Dangling, legs thrashing, tiptoes barely touching. The men hold various implements of torture. One holds a bullwhip, two have cattle prods, one holds an enormous knife.

God, please let this end soon. Please let us just die.

Next they open my cage door. I don't want to be shocked with the cattle prod, so I crawl out, cursing under my breath. *Cataha* himself is standing by my door, and he grabs me by the hair, hauls me to my feet, and marches me over to the chair.

They treated me differently. I wasn't kicked to the floor, I wasn't stripped. Why?

"Tell me your real name. I want to hear it from your lips." *Cataha's* voice is creaky and strange.

"Fuck yourself!" I shout at him.

One of the men slashes at Darya with the whip, leaving a vicious red stripe across her stomach, and she jerks and makes a strangled sound. Tears run down her face. I can almost feel the agony of the whip on my own skin, and I can't imagine what it cost her not to cry out. She'll be screaming soon enough. She won't be able to help it, no matter how strong she is. She's only flesh.

"Stop it!" I cry. "Why are you hitting her? I'm the one who's not talking! Hit me!"

But I'm an idiot. This is exactly how these men operate. They find out what will hurt you the most, and attack you that way.

"Your real name!" *Cataha* barks again.

Before I can answer, the man whips Darya again, and this time she screams and her body convulses. Her eyes are open wide, huge with terror.

I meet his gaze. I am sure that my answer spells my doom, but I am doomed anyway. "My name is Willow Toporov."

Cataha gestures at the man with the whip, and the man lowers his arm. They lower Darya to the ground, so she's sagging on the chain, her feet on the floor, her head hanging down.

Cataha pulls his mask off and steps closer to me. He's bathed in the harsh white lights. His face is strangely, horribly familiar.

The hair is different than I remember. Clipped close and bleached a pale blonde. He has facial hair – a goatee. The nose is a different shape. His cheekbones are wider and higher, his jaw broader. He has brown eyes, which must be contact lenses.

I know this. I know his eyes are really blue. I know his hair used to be black and curly. Because despite all the plastic surgery, the distorted face, the scars...this is Vasily Toporov.

This is my adoptive father. The man who died, right next to my mother, when I was seventeen years old, when their small private plane fell from the sky. He's come back from Hell, to drag me down with him.

The look of hatred that's twisting his face is terrifying.

His head jerks to the side. He screams at someone I can't see. "It's her! Shut up, shut up, shut up! I brought her back!"

Who the hell is he talking to? I can't see anyone, although my eyes haven't fully adjusted to the light in this room. Maybe there's a one-way mirror I can't see, or a hidden video camera.

"I'm the one you want," I plead. "Not Darya. Please let her go, and I'll do anything you want. If you hurt her, I'll make you kill me."

He lunges at me, hands closing around my throat, squeezing hard.

"Let her go, you fucking pig!" Darya howls. So brave. So foolish.

One of the men slashes her with the whip again, and she screams so hard I think my eardrums will split.

My vision is turning black, and I'm frantic for air. I claw at his hands, my lungs burning.

"You treacherous bitch," Vasily rasps. "You backstabbing little traitor whore. You're the reason that your mother's dead. And I'm going to make you pay for it."

CHAPTER NINETEEN

Day fifteen...
SERGEI

I'm back at my house in Russia, ready to explode out of my own skin.

The rage that boils inside is killing me, burning me from the inside out. I haven't slept all night, but I'm not tired. I'm filled with maddening energy, frantic, desperate to slash and maim and kill.

My Willow is gone. She was snatched from the bridal shop in Sweden yesterday morning, and I have no idea where on the planet she might be, or what's being done to her.

I thought I'd taken sufficient precautions to keep her safe. I'd stationed two of my best men behind the shop. Honestly, at the time I was more worried that she'd try to make a run for it, that she'd leave me.

I didn't anticipate Ludmilla's betrayal. I still don't know why she did it, but I will find out and I will make her pay in blood and screams before she dies at my hand.

It makes no sense; I know she resented Willow because of who her family was, but how could she have hated her enough to make a deal with the actual devil? How could she have thought she'd survive my wrath? All the money in the world won't protect her from me when I find her.

I'm turning the events of yesterday over in my mind again and again, a horror movie I can't stop watching.

When the men I had stationed in the alley failed to check in on their radios, we rushed into the shop. It was too late. She'd been taken.

While my men and I scoured the streets, I had my security team hack into the city's system of public safety cameras. Ludmilla and two men dragged Willow out of the back alley and stuffed her into the back of a dark van. The van was last seen heading to a small private airport.

At first I thought we'd find her easily. We followed the GPS transmitter, and flew to Russia in my private plane. As we flew, I was assembling my troops.

I called in every man I could get, and by late that afternoon, we were headed to a remote warehouse on the outskirts of a tiny abandoned village. It made sense that he'd take her there. I wanted to believe it so badly.

There were at least thirty men outside the warehouse, patrolling, wearing body armor. I had a hundred and twenty. We were better armed, and we came at them from all directions.

We stormed them with everything we had. Snipers, grenade launchers, Vityaz-SN submachine guns, stun grenades.

We didn't bother with trying the doors. We identified the location of the GPS tracker in the building and blasted open a wall on the opposite side, then we filled the interior of the building with tear-gas. My men went rolling in, wearing masks, clearing rooms.

I was on the outside with the snipers, armed with a Lobaev TSLV-8 rifle, taking out a few remaining men who were shooting at us from camouflaged positions in the woods. We eliminated them quickly, and their screams were swallowed by the wind that whipped through the trees.

With the last of them dead, we hurried towards the building, pushing through ankle-deep snow in our heavy ceramic plate body armor. Hope flared inside me, but just as quickly died as I glanced around me. Something was wrong.

"This is too easy," I muttered to Slavik. Slavik shouldn't have come; he still wasn't sufficiently recovered, but he'd insisted.

"You call this easy?" He gestured around us. The air stank of blood and gunpowder. Some of our men were being carried away on stretchers; a few of them were in body bags. Their families would be richly rewarded.

"For *Cataha*? Yes."

Slavik and eight other men moved with me.

I've always been capable of waiting. I've always been good at strategy, at thinking ahead. Not today. I wanted to scream with impatience, to rush in full speed, but outside the building, the faint scent of teargas stung our eyes. We quickly clapped on our masks and headed in. We stepped over rubble and bodies, moving to the back of the building where we'd picked up the signal.

Andrei called out to us, and his words chilled my blood. "Not picking up any heat signatures inside. Nothing alive here," he yelled. He and his men were equipped with thermal imaging cameras.

I stormed towards his voice, nearly mad with rage and

terror. The GPS sensor had led us there, and if there was no heat signature...*Willow must be dead.*

I moved into another world, a world of ice and hate.

At the back of the warehouse, I smashed the lock on a door with the butt of my gun and kicked the door open. My men were shouting at me, Alexei screaming, "Wait, wait, let me clear the room!" His voice was muffled by his teargas mask. I couldn't have stopped if I'd wanted to. My body, my brain, were screaming, *Willow, Willow, Willow!*

I barreled into the room like a tank, with my men on my heels.

And we found not one but three women, sprawled on the ground. Their blood stained the concrete floor in Rorschach splatters of horror. Not only had their faces been mutilated beyond recognition, but they'd all been gutted.

The winds of the steppes howled in my ears as I stormed towards their bodies. Time stopped and sound faded.

I'd gone sociopathic, with no access to my feelings.

I knew what to look for, to tell if one of these tortured creatures was my Willow.

I looked at the women, picturing their last moments on Earth when they knew all hope was gone and prayed for death as a release, and I staggered back.

"Sir..." Slavik's voice was a million miles away. "Sir...is it..."

"None of them are Willow." I dragged myself back to Earth. "He planted the GPS here. He's doing this to fuck with us." I looked at him, with blazing eyes. I grabbed his arm in a crushing grip. "We. Have. To. Find. Her."

WILLOW

"Leave me alone! Shut up, you bitch, shut up!" Vasily drops his hands and staggers backwards, and I gasp for air, drawing it in in heaving gulps. He has his hands over his ears. *Who is he talking to?*

Then he gestures at one of his men, who produces a water bottle. The man shoves it against my lips, and I take several gulps before he pulls it away.

"Please give some to her?" I beg.

He glances at Vasily, who screams, "Fine. Fine!"

But Vasily's not talking to his guard; he's staring into space as he yells. I swear it looks as if he's talking to a ghost that only he can see. The man looks worried as he walks over and lets Darya have several sips of water.

Vasily is alive.

I'm struggling for words. I want to scream, threaten, insult. But I'm in a room full of armed men and I don't want him to murder me and Darya.

"Father." I make myself say that lie out loud. "Please. Why are you doing this to me?"

"You have betrayed me. You've been sleeping with the enemy."

I glare at him. *You're the enemy,* I think, but I don't say it out loud. Darya's life depends on it. "Your brother sold me to him."

He nods, his eyes snapping with rage. "Yes. That weakling piece of shit. I should have killed him when we were in kindergarten."

Well, isn't that special?

"Please let Darya go." I try to keep my voice gentle.

He slaps me across the face so hard that I cry out, almost falling off the chair.

I'm sick with fear. He's acting like a crazy man. He was

always an angry control freak, but he was never like this before. The wild mood swings, the bizarre screaming at...nothing?

"Do you know what you've done to me?" he howls.

Tears are running down my cheeks. "I haven't done anything to you! I didn't even know you were alive! I haven't seen you in six years!"

"You turned your mother against me! She was going to betray me – for you!"

Fear clutches at my throat. *Yes, she was. How much does he know?*

He begins pacing. His eyes are mad.

"She was the perfect woman. She was everything a wife should be. She lived her life for me; she lived only to please me."

Yes, because you were a horrifying sociopath and she had no other choice.

"I didn't even want a child to ruin our perfect paradise. But she did, so I got you." He whirls to face me, his lips twisting in a malicious leer. "You're not mine, did you know that? I bought you. You came cheap, too. You're the daughter of a cocksucking whore."

"Yes. I know. Sergei told me." Then I feel a stab of fear. Should I even have said Sergei's name?

But for the moment, Vasily has resumed his crazy pacing, and he's not looking at me. He stares at the floor. "Your mother loved you. That's the only reason you're not dead right now."

How is he even here? "You...you were on the plane with my mother. And the plane went down. What happened?"

His mad eyes bulge. "My enemies were closing in on all sides. I had been planning to disappear for years." He's ranting at the wall. "I was going to take you and your mother with me, and we'd hide out and let the world forget about us. Start over. Live on our own for a few years. Marry you to a man who'd give us a dowry fit for a queen, a man who'd teach you respect. Build our empire anew. But that whore betrayed me. She chose you over me, you little *bitch!* She was going to take you and run. She was going to leave me!"

My blood turns to ice.

I always believed that our family's enemies blew up the small private plane that he and my mother were on. Now I know.

Vasily murdered my mother – my sweet, lovely mother – out of jealousy. He must have put someone else on the plane to take his place. The bodies were burned beyond recognition. They identified my mother by some of her melted jewelry.

Rage flares up inside me like a flash fire. It burns all rational thought from my mind.

I don't care that I'm a prisoner. I don't care about myself or Darya or the armed men pacing the floor, or the fact that there's no way for me to escape from this place.

He killed my mother. Because of me. Because she tried to protect me.

She died in a fireball of agony and fear, murdered by her husband.

I rush towards him, screaming with rage. The world turns red. I claw at his face with my acrylic nails – the last weapon I have left.

Someone zaps me with a cattle prod, and my body convulses. I fall to the ground, crying out, legs thrashing. I bang my head on the concrete when I fall, and blackness descends. I'm hit with the cattle prod again, and my whole body is on fire. I'm kicking and flailing; I've lost all control of my body.

My father's voice has gone high pitched, shrieking at me. The words ride over my body in waves of agony.

Bitch, whore...betrayer...

My head explodes and I'm gone, gone, gone...

CHAPTER TWENTY

Day fifteen...

I don't want to be awake.

I don't want to be in this world.

Darya and I spend the night in our cages, burning with thirst and sick with hunger and fear. We lie there curled up with our blankets pulled around us, not speaking. We don't have the energy to talk. I'm so exhausted that sometimes I drift off, but then I wake up with a jerk and the nightmare reality washes over me, threatening to drown me in terror.

I have to squat over the bucket to pee, and I'm so dizzy I almost fall over. Then I crawl back to my mattress and pull the blanket over myself.

I want to think about better times, about sunshine and Sergei and my family, but it's hard to think about anything except how thirsty and terrified I am. My head still aches from where Vasily hit me, my leg throbs where the GPS tracker was removed and it was inexpertly stitched back up.

When things are pleasurable, when life is going well, time rushes by at the speed of a freight train. I never stopped to appreciate the good times. Now I'll never feel pleasure or warmth again, and every miserable second feels like a century. I can't believe how long this horrible night has lasted.

When I'm ready to sink into despair, I force myself to remember the girls I've saved. The girls and the children Sergei has saved. I hurt Vasily, at least a little.

I wish I could have saved Darya.

When the sun rises, shining through the tiny window in our room, a guard throws open the door and we both flinch when he approaches.

Is this the end?

But we are given hunks of bread and one bottle of water each, shoved through the bars of our cages. He leaves without a backward glance, because we're beneath his notice, like livestock. We gnaw the bread like animals and gulp the water down. It might be our last meal.

Just as we're finishing, two guards come for us and open our cages. Darya and I are both hunched in on ourselves, staring down at the floor as we're hustled down a hallway and into a room that's the pit of the damned.

The chemical stink is stronger here. There's a blinding light overhead, illuminating this hellscape. Two more guards are there, standing by the doors. There are naked women chained down to tables. I count six. Legs spread so wide it's painful just to look at them. They're mostly silent, a couple of them sobbing quietly. There's a hopeless, broken quality to their sobs that chills my blood. There are two empty tables.

One of the men orders Darya to strip, and she glares at him but obeys. Fighting would just turn him on.

He pushes her over to an empty table and makes her lie down on it, face up. She lies perfectly still as he spreads her legs and fixes each ankle to a corner of the table, then does the same to her wrists. Most of the fight's gone out of her. And me too. I'm too exhausted and weak to fight right now. I'm sure that's why they have us half-starved and exhausted – to make us easier to manage.

And because that's the kind of thing that turns these men on.

Other than the tables, the room is mostly bare, with some metal cabinets and a sink against one wall. A few chains dangle from the ceiling overhead, which apparently is standard torture equipment here.

"Willow. Willow. Can you help me?" a familiar voice husks from one of the tables, and when I walk over, I'm shocked to see that it's Ludmilla. Her face is bruised and puffy, her lips cracked and bleeding.

"What the hell happened to you?" I ask bitterly. "And no, I can't help you. I can't even help myself."

She stares at me in misery. "Your father. He's *Cataha*. And he's the man who took my sister. I didn't know." She hiccups a sob. "When I made the deal with him...I didn't know who he was. Everyone thought your father was dead. But he's alive. He's the devil come back to life."

"Yes." I intone the word without emotion.

"My sister...Sabina...she's worse than dead. I wish she was dead. She's became the mistress of a wealthy sadist named Mogens. She helps him train slaves." Ludmilla's eyes are vacant with shock. "*Cataha*, your father, he brought her in here and she spit in my face. She's gone mad. She's the same as they are now. He did that just to hurt me! It's worse than them killing her."

She twists her head to look at me with haunted eyes. "We used to play dress-up. We used to walk to school together holding hands. She was my shadow; she followed me everywhere, copied everything I did. And now she doesn't care that I'm going to be raped and murdered. How did this happen?"

I narrow my eyes, refusing to offer her any comfort. "I wish I could say I'm sorry, but you betrayed me, and Darya, and everything you stood for. You could have helped Sergei catch my father, and instead you stabbed us in the back."

One of the women twists her head to look at me. There's a bruise on her cheekbone. Her ebony hair is plastered to her forehead with sweat. The look in her eyes makes me want to weep. She's abandoned all hope. She's muttering something to herself over and over. "I'm a stupid whore. I'm a stupid whore."

Despair wells up in me. I want to rip those chains off her. I want to rush her to a hospital. I want to tell her that she's all right, that she's safe, that nobody will ever hurt her again...but that's not what's going to happen.

She's going to die, just like I am.

I walk away. The guards are watching me, eyes burning with contempt and cruelty, fingering their weapons.

Vasily barrels through the door, and they all tense up. He's muttering to himself as if he's having a secret conversation that only he can hear.

His men look uneasy. Is there any way that I could use that? Not with him right there, but maybe at some point. I'm desperate. I'll try anything.

My adopter, my tormentor, walks up to me, and I stiffen and brace myself for whatever horror he's going to throw at me.

I look into his eyes and see a howling wasteland. Sanity left there long ago.

"I want to kill you, but she won't let me," he whines. "Your mother doesn't want me to kill you. She said so. She talks to me, you know? Does she talk to you?"

It hits me like a hammer blow. *So that's who he thinks is talking to him.* The guilt has driven him mad.

"No, never." *Because you took her from me, you psychotic son of a bitch. Because she's dead.*

He gloats at that. "I knew it. She talks to me and not you. She always loved me more."

"I know it. I know she did." It's not true at all, but I'll say anything to placate this lunatic. "But this is between me and you. Please let these women go," I plead. "My mother was kind and gentle – she wouldn't have wanted you to hurt anyone. Please don't desecrate her memory like this."

He doesn't seem to hear me. "Since your mother doesn't want me to kill you, I'll give you a chance. One more chance. Prove you're worthy of me. You can work with me. By my side. Are you strong enough to be a Toporov? Do you deserve the name?"

Do I deserve the name of a rapist and murderer? I strangle on a laugh of disbelief and horror. But he's deadly serious.

He points at the women, and his lips stretch back into a hideous rictus grin. "You and me. We're working together."

I'm stunned into silence.

He can't possibly mean this. It's insane. But then, so is he.

He looks back at me with a sly smile. "Do you want to hear about my operation?"

No. Hell no.

"Yes," I whisper. "Please tell me about it."

He starts walking towards the women on the tables, and reluctantly, I follow him. He waves his hand at them. "I have collected all these women over the course of the last few weeks. Not just the ones in here; we've got more in the back. Twenty-seven in all. Selected for their youth and beauty. We get them from nightclubs, and from a fake employment agency I have set up."

I wince as I look at them, seeing the misery and despair on their faces. They're thinking about how foolish they were, desperately wishing they could go back in time and do things differently. Wishing they were anywhere but here. Praying to wake up from this nightmare, and knowing they never will.

Vasily shakes his head in disgust as he looks at them. "Only four of them were virgins, I'm afraid. Women are such whores today."

He falls silent, looking at me expectantly. "That's unfortunate," I murmur, instead of spewing venom in his face, shouting insults and threats.

But words are useless against him. I need a weapon. Something to cut him open, to make him pay for the agony he's dealt out over the years, to make life a little fairer.

Maybe if I play along, I can get my hands on one.

Vasily rambles on, like a businessman giving a tour of a factory. "I've got buyers coming in two days. I've worked with them over the years, and they know I only sell the highest quality merchandise. They'll pay to sample the wares, except for the virgins of course. Then they'll pay me a fat fee for the slaves of their choice, and fly on home with them. Millions and millions of dollars. And I do this every month. I'm the go-to man in the whole region." Sweat beads on his forehead as he brags to me.

I can't believe how much he's changed since I last saw him. He was haughty before, yes, but this is more like mania. Killing my mother has clearly eaten away at him, and I take at least some small comfort from that.

"I can see that you've got a highly profitable business here. Can you please let Darya go?" I ask him quietly, keeping my tone humble and my eyes cast down, the way I did when I was a teenager and he was my father. "Darya could work with you too. She's worked in an office before." Total lie, but I'll say anything at this point. "I could...I could balance your books for you. I'm great at that. She could help me."

He throws back his head and laughs, a horrible rasping sound.

"Are you really that fucking stupid? No. If you want to work with me, you have to prove yourself. My men are bored. I brought these bitches in here to keep them amused. So you're going to pick which one they fuck first."

"What?" I suck in a gasp of horror. "I...I can't do that! That's not helping you run your business! I mean...if you hurt the women, they won't be worth as much..."

"I knew you weren't worthy. I knew it." Now his voice is a high-pitched whine. He points at Darya. "So we'll take your little friend. I hate to waste a virgin, because they're worth so much more, but you leave me no choice."

What kind of sick logic is that?

Darya jerks at her restraints. His men start walking towards her, unzipping their pants, and her eyes widen in horror. She bites her lip and stares at the ceiling, her body as tense as a drawn bowstring.

"No! Ludmilla! Take Ludmilla!" I cry.

A nasty smile twists his lips. "Good, good. You're coming around. Why Ludmilla?"

I sway where I stand, fighting not to weep. I make my mouth form words. "She...she betrayed me."

"Yesss...." It comes out as a hiss of satisfaction. "Thinking like a Toporov. Yes. Very good."

And his men line up as Ludmilla cries out and thrashes, struggling against her chains. The first man in line unzips his pants and climbs onto the table, on top of her. Then he spits on her face.

"Ugly old cunt," he sneers at her. "Don't think you make my dick hard, bitch. I'm just following orders."

I hug myself and turn away. I can't believe I just did that. I can't believe I just pointed someone out and ordered their rape. Ludmilla is shrieking as the man slams into her and the other guards, five of them, jeer and caw insults. Her body jerks on the table.

I'm sick. I'm so angry I want to burn them all alive. I'm shaking with horror. Darya is still strapped down, legs splayed open, and some of the men are glancing her way. She's the prettiest girl in the room. How much longer can I keep her from being molested?

After the first man finishes with Ludmilla, he slides off, and a second man replaces him. Ludmilla lets out a hoarse cry of pain as he rams into her.

I can't stand it anymore. "Please stop this!" I cry. "My mother doesn't want it! She – she just told me so!"

Instantly, he's mad with rage. "Liar! Liar! You said she doesn't talk to you! Liar, liar, liar!"

He lashes out with his fist, and I hear my nose crunch and break, and there's a split second when I don't feel anything. Then the explosion of pain drives me to my knees, and I'm gagging on my own blood. The room wheels around me, and I vomit on the floor.

"No, no, no!" Through a haze of agony, I can hear Vasily's tormented shrieks. "I had to! She talked back to me! She lied! That's against the rules! You know the rules! I taught you the rules! Shut up, shut up, shut up!"

Then he snuffles pathetically.

"Fine. Fine. Fine. Fine. Fine. I'll give her another chance. You hear me? Fine. Fine. Fine. Fine."

Two of his guards haul me from the room and take me down the hallway into a room that's been set up like a doctor's office.

I collapse on a chair, head whirling.

A white-coated man in his forties comes in a few minutes later, and I sit stock-still as he carefully cleans up the blood and splints my nose.

My head throbs in pain. I feel nauseous and dizzy.

The doctor helps me sit up.

"When you went to medical school, did you think you'd end up going into business with men who torture women?" I ask him, my dry, cracked lips curling in scorn. "Your mother must be so proud."

"I thought I'd be earning more money. And now I am," he growls, and gives me a glass of water and two pills. "Antibiotics, painkillers."

My hands are shaking so hard that he has to help me take the pills, and hold the glass. I gulp it all down, and then I'm allowed to use a bathroom.

A guard brings me in a roast beef sandwich, and I'm in so much pain I'm nauseous, but I force myself to eat.

And then I'm hustled back to my cage. Darya is already there, curled up, blanket wrapped around her.

"They put their fingers in me," she chokes out. "But then your father made them stop because he says he'll get more money for me if I'm still a virgin. He hit one of them on the head with his gun."

"I'm sorry," I mumble, my voice sounding strange and nasal because of my broken nose. "I'm so sorry."

"It's not your fault." It comes out as a long, sad sigh. "I think I'm going to try to sleep now." And she turns her back to me.

This cage is my life, and my life is now hell.

CHAPTER TWENTY-ONE

Day sixteen...
SERGEI

It's dawn, and my office is a shambles. I've torn it apart, thrown everything that's not nailed down at the walls. Books ripped to shreds, papers scattered across the floor, pillows torn open. With every step, broken glass crunches under my feet.

I still haven't slept. At least I don't think I have. I'm moving in a daze of horror and rage.

It's starting to sink in. I might never see her again.

I've put out the word. Fifty million dollars for my Willow's safe return. Death to whoever took her, or knows where she is and does not tell me immediately. The kind of death that I specialize in – slow, excruciating.

Nobody has contacted me and asked for ransom. Nobody has called me up to taunt me. This makes no sense. *Cataha* is the type to gloat.

Why haven't I heard from him?

I have my entire network on this. I'm offering a fortune. We're getting some information trickling in about men who work for *Cataha*, called to work with him on a special project, but they were just ordered to get in a truck. No idea where they were headed.

The special project is Willow.

I know it.

This is what I tried to save her from. This is why I was willing to break her heart, stomp on it, slash it to pieces, back in California.

Why I was willing to break my own heart by lying to her.

Yes, I have a heart. I know this now. It beats only for Willow.

Hurting her was better than the alternative – whatever's happening to her right this minute, somewhere dark and terrifying. Where she's all alone and I can't protect her.

And it's her fault too. Damn her and her morals. Her conscience. What is the purpose of a conscience? What good has a conscience ever done for anyone? A conscience does nothing but mock and torment and insult.

Her conscience will be the death of her.

No. She can't die. If she dies, I'll burn the world down. Nobody will be safe. Good or evil, innocent or tainted, I will make everyone suffer for my loss.

Then Slavik bursts through the door, his face stubbled with beard growth and his eyes bloodshot. He was out all night, personally breaking down the doors of anyone who might possibly have a lead on *Cataha*'s whereabouts.

"What the fuck?" I snarl at him.

"Andrei's got news. He has a lead."

As Slavik explains, I feel a wild surge of hope. Andrei's waiting for me at a construction site that I own.

I round up my men and we tear through the streets to get there. His lead is a woman named Sabina. Ludmilla's sister. And she's one of those vile bitches who betrays her own sex by luring women into the sex trade with false promises.

We're there within the hour. Andrei will be getting a fat bonus from me.

The site has been closed down for the day, all the workers sent home. Andrei's there with a dozen men. He meets me outside the room where they've got her chained up, and explains the situation to me. And he's got a task for Slavik.

I storm into the room where my men are holding Sabina, who is strapped down to a chair. She was taken eight years ago, when she was sixteen. She looks much older than her years now, with that hardened prettiness so common to women in the game. Her lips are puffy with silicone, her hair is bleached a frosty platinum and blow-dried straight, and she's dressed in Gucci from head to toe.

The look of rage and contempt twisting her face shows that she's too stupid to understand her situation. Andrei has helpfully laid out a row of tools on a table right where she can see it – pliers, a blowtorch, skinning knives – but I can tell she doesn't believe that I'd use them. She's about to find out that I live up to my reputation.

She spits at me when I approach, a glob of saliva landing on my jacket. "I don't know a fucking thing about your stupid whore girlfriend, and my boyfriend's going to cut your dick off and feed it to you, asshole!" she sneers. "If you were smart, you'd—"

I never get to find out what I would do if I were smart. As she's screeching at me, I pull a knife from my waistband and slash it down the left side of her face, carving a straight red line from cheekbone to chin.

Her eyes fly open with shock, and she makes a strangling noise, then starts screaming.

"My face! My face! My faaaaace!" She's a cartoon caricature of shock and horror. She can't believe it. I've seen that look so many times before, on people sitting in chairs just like this one, as the horrible reality of what I'm about to do to them finally starts to penetrate their dumb brains.

"Wasn't anything special to begin with. I'm going to cut those silicone lips off and feed them to you."

I ball up my fist and punch her on the side of the head. I have to will myself to pull my punch so I don't snap her neck. Her head rocks to the side and her eyes go unfocused for a second.

Now she's crying hysterically, straining against her bonds, taking in huge gulps of air and making *huh, huh, huh* sounds. Gritty rivers of mascara stream down her cheeks and mingle with the blood that's dripping onto her white sweater.

"Where is she?" I bellow, pressing my knife up against her unmarked cheek. It's taking everything I have not to gut her right there. I crave the sound of her agonized screams. My hand is twitching, my arm vibrating from the effort of not killing her.

I'm never this impatient, but the stakes have never been this high. Every second that she keeps this information from me is another second that Willow is suffering. Maybe dying.

Slavik bangs open the door, carrying a brown cardboard box, and instantly the room fills with the stink of blood. Much stronger than the little trickle that's running down Sabina's cheek.

Sabina still doesn't get it. "Do you idiots even know who my boyfriend is?" Her voice is an outraged, terrified screech. Half-whining, half threatening. It's really important to her

that we know who her boyfriend is, because all her impor-
tance and self-esteem are wrapped up in her identity as
Mogens' Girlfriend.

Yes, I know who he is. Mogens is a medium-level pimp
with sadistic tendencies, inefficient security, and delusions
of grandeur, and most of his men will be dead by the end of
the day, at the hands of my people.

"This boyfriend?" Slavik says helpfully, and he reaches
into the box. He carried out the task that Andrei gave him
with admirable speed and efficiency.

Because when Andrei was grabbing Sabina, some of my
other men were grabbing Mogens, and they brought him to
the same construction site.

Sabina stares at the box, and she's finally starting to wise
up. This time, it only takes her a split second to figure out
what's coming.

"Nooo..."

Slavik reaches in, grabs a handful of Mogen's hair, and
pulls his head out of the box. He's raggedly sawed it off just
under the chin. Mogen's mouth gapes open, and one of his
eyes is closed, the other open and staring at nothing. The
smell of blood is overpowering, the reek so strong that I can
taste it when I breathe.

Sabina screams at the top of her lungs, ridiculous melo-
dramatic horror movie screams, and then her eyes roll back
in her head and she passes out. Her head lolls to the side.

A bucket of ice-cold water wakes her right back up.
Andrei had it sitting nearby. He's thought of everything.

She jerks upright, and now terror has torn her face
apart. She's not pretty at all anymore. She blubbers and
squeaks. "Don't kill me, no, no, pleaaaase..."

I grab the tin snippers off the table and pinch her nose
with them, squeezing hard. Now she's talking, words

spilling over each other, desperate to tell me everything I want to know.

She was taken to the place where they were holding Ludmilla, *Cataha's* current base of operations. She got the impression that was where they'd be taking Willow.

They made her put a hood over her head, and she could tell they were doubling back on their tracks as they drove, but it took a total of about three hours to get there, which at least narrows things down. At one point, she smelled smoke from a peat fire, which narrows it down even more. The peat bogs in Russia sometimes catch fire and burn uncontrollably for months or years, and there's a notorious one in our district.

They drove for half an hour after she smelled the smoke. The inside of the building looked like an old warehouse, and some rooms had factory equipment, but there was dust and cobwebs in the area she was in, so she knew that the factory hadn't been operating for a while. She smelled a weird chemical smell.

Andrei is listening to everything she says and frantically tapping on a laptop on a small table.

Then she says something that fills me with more rage than I thought my body could contain.

She claims that *Cataha* is Vasily Toporov.

My tormentor, Willow's father. That piece of shit who was supposed to have died years ago. The man who was there to greet me and my brother at the orphanage the day we were dragged in there screaming.

The man who stood there while our clothes were cut from our bodies. Who watched as we were forcibly bent over tables and probed, our ass cheeks spread as men jammed their fingers up there to see exactly how tight we were.

The man whose lips curled in a smile as they dragged Pyotr away from me, his screams of terror piercing my heart.

The blackness, which I thought was gone, is back now, and I'm roaring with fury.

Deep in the dark, I hear Pyotr's cries the first time a man takes him, shrieks of pure agony as he's torn apart by some pervert's dick. I feel the savage blows of men's fists raining down on me as I struggle to get to him. I hear my own weak, pathetic cries. "Please, take me instead! Do it to me instead!"

I'm blind and deaf, the sounds of my shouts coming from so far away they're like an echo. I don't know how much time has passed.

When I come to, I'm looking down on the ruined pulp of Sabina's face, and from the angle that her head is hanging at, she can't be alive.

And the full horror of what I've done hits me so hard that I stagger backwards and almost fall.

I beat her to death.

And she was my only link to Willow.

"No!" I shout. "No, no, no!" I look around wildly. Slavik's mouth is bleeding.

I must have hit him.

There are six other men there. Andrei is hunched over his computer, his fingers clacking frantically.

"I'm searching property records," he calls out to me.

I'm shaking all over. I've lost it. I've ruined everything. I've just killed Willow as surely as if I pulled the trigger on a pistol pressed to her skull.

Slavik slaps me across the face so hard that I stagger, and I lunge for his throat. Instantly, all six men are on me, three on each side, and they grab me by the arms and barely manage to restrain me.

Slavik doesn't flinch. He's in my face, flushed with fury and bellowing.

"Get it the *fuck* together!" he shouts at me. "You little bitch! Stop being a fucking pussy! Who the hell are you? Are you Sergei Volkov, or are you a weak little girl on her period?"

I draw on every ounce of strength I have and I force myself to go still. My men release me and step away, watching me warily.

"Where are we?" I say to Andrei.

He twists around to look at me. "Sir, we've got something. We've got something! We just got an email, and you will not believe who it's from!"

CHAPTER TWENTY-TWO

Day sixteen...
WILLOW

Even with the pain pills that the doctor gave me again this morning, my face throbs with pain, and I'm so sick and weak I can barely stand. I can't breathe through my nose, which is crusted with blood. My hair is greasy and matted.

And Vasily doesn't look much better than I do. He hasn't shaved, and his white button-down shirt has yellow pit stains. We're back in the room where they bring the women they want to rape.

Now there are only two of them. Darya and Ludmilla. The tables are about ten feet apart.

Ludmilla is a mass of bruises, splattered across her like a gruesome abstract painting.

Darya's cough is worse, racking her body. She's shivering uncontrollably in the chill air. Neither one of us is going to last much longer here.

Vasily's men are nervous, biting their lips, sneaking glances at him and at each other. They follow a leader who's going mad in front of their eyes, and they're royally screwed. *Cataha* has made enemies everywhere, and anyone who is gunning for him will be gunning for them. And he's barely holding on to sanity by a thread, so where will that leave them when he finally snaps?

There's got to be a way I can use this.

But when I glance from guard to guard, when I try to catch their eyes, they all glare and avoid any connection to my gaze.

Vasily rolls a cart towards me. When I see what's on it, sick terror floods through my body. There are knives, and a jar of some yellowish liquid. He opens the jar and sets the top down on the tray, and even through my clogged nose, I catch a whiff of something so acrid that it must be acid.

"Last chance," he rasps at me. "Prove you're worthy to work by my side. These aren't women, they're livestock. In this business, you need to be able to eliminate some of the livestock at any time. To set an example for the others, or because the livestock isn't following orders, or the livestock tried to escape. Livestock can be replaced. So which one are you going to eliminate today?"

This is an evil, horrible choice. I didn't think I had any tears left, but tears fill my eyes and spill onto my cheeks.

Ludmilla. It's going to have to be her.

Slowly, I approach, and as I draw close to her I suck in a gasp of horror. *One of her ears has been sliced off.* Her face is swollen and puffy from beatings, and her mouth is agape, her eyes blank with shock.

She'd bedeviled *Cataha's* operation, threatened it, exposed it, and now he's taking his revenge.

I lean down.

"I'm sorry," I whisper to her. And I am. I can't even summon the strength to be angry with her anymore. I'm just deeply sad.

She looks up at me, and she husks out words that I don't understand at first. "The weather is so bad today."

That was the code-phrase we developed when I was helping girls escape traffickers.

It means help is on the way.

But that's not possible.

If there's one thing I'm sure of, it's that Vasily did not ever give her the opportunity to call for help.

She's hallucinating from pain and fear and shock. That's the only explanation.

"I'm sorry," I say to her again, choking on a sob.

I look at Vasily. "I pick Ludmilla. Give me a gun."

Please, please be that stupid.

But instead he grabs a knife and pushes it into my hand.

"Why are you so weak? Did I raise you to be this weak?" He hauls off and slaps me, and my face explodes in agony, my nose throbbing anew. Tears of pain leak from my eyes and dribble down my cheeks.

My vision blurring, I cast a frantic glance at the guards. They're standing there, impassive, stone-faced.

"How long are you going to follow a lunatic?" I shout at them, desperate, clenching the knife in my shaking hand. "He'll lead you to your deaths!"

They ignore me.

Vasily punches me in the stomach so hard that I double over and drop the knife. He kicks me in the ribs, savagely, with his steel-toed boots. Every square inch of me pulses with pain. The room is spinning around me so fast that I vomit on the floor.

Then he grabs the knife.

"Say goodbye to your little friend!" His voice goes high and mad. He lets out a hysterical giggle. "Get it? From the movie?"

He moves towards Darya.

I pull up the last of my strength from somewhere deep inside me. I push through the pain and dizziness and stagger to my feet. "No!" I cry, my voice weak and wavery. I snatch the knife from him and stumble towards Ludmilla.

"Yes! Yes!" Vasily crows in triumph. "Gut her like a fish!"

I sway where I stand. Vasily has strangled time. It has slowed to a hideous crawl. Every second lasts forever.

The room is dead silent, except for the muffled sound of Darya's sobs. Ludmilla's eyes are vacant, her mouth slack. I don't think she's even conscious anymore.

I have to do this. It's the only way to save Darya. Ludmilla's dead anyway.

Horror floods through me, and I barely feel human. Instead of gutting Ludmilla, I force myself to slash her neck, slicing cleanly through her carotid artery. She jerks back to consciousness. I'm screaming as I do it.

Her gurgling cries destroy me, and I fall to my knees. "No, no, no!" I'm wailing. But I was the one who did it. I was the one who held the knife.

"You fucking bitch! Too easy, too easy! She needed to *suffer!*" Vasily lunges at me and grabs me by the throat. I drop the knife and my vision goes red. I'm so weak that I can barely slap at his hands.

Then he lets go and he's spinning around in circles. Like a bloody lunatic. He claps his hands over his ears and shuts his eyes. "Just let me kill her! She's a bitch, she's a whore, she's a traitor! It's your fault she's dead!"

He thinks my mother is speaking to him right here, right now. It's enough to make me believe in ghosts. If my mother were a ghost, this is what she'd do. Torment him. Protect me.

The thought makes me sob even harder.

Sergei. Sergei. Come for me. Please.

I swear I can almost feel him near me. I've sensed it in the past. I've known when he was near me. Could he be here, in this dark place?

I make myself climb to my feet. I'm dizzy, I'm sick, I hurt all over, but fear is draining away from me now. I think I'm in shock.

I stagger towards the tray, reaching for the weapons. I need a knife. I will kill Vasily, and consequences be damned. We're all dead here anyway.

As I fumble for a knife, Vasily lunges for the jar of acid and grabs it. He runs over to Darya and flings it at her face. It sizzles and bubbles on her skin, and she makes a sound that I've near heard before, a scream of pure agony that rips me in two. Her body convulses on the table. The right side of her face is burning.

"Call the doctor, call the doctor!" I cry out to Vasily. I've got a knife in my hand again, but the room is full of armed men, and if I stab him, they'll come after me and they won't help Darya. *"My mother wants you to call the doctor!"*

"Did she talk to you?" His eyes are wild. "Right now? What did she say?"

I force myself to mouth a lie that makes me sick. "She said she loves you."

He nods eagerly. "What else?"

"She wants you to get help for Darya!"

Darya isn't screaming anymore. Why isn't she screaming? She's gone limp. Is she dead? I can't think that she's dead; I won't accept it.

"Lies!" he shrieks at me.

Vasily falls to his knees and hugs himself, rocking and wailing.

"Liar! Liar! Liar! She would never say that! She wouldn't dare!" he hisses. He stares at me. "Make her come back! Make her be here! Bring her back!" His eyes are wild with hope, as if I could actually do such a thing.

Vasily's men are muttering among themselves.

I call out to them, desperate. "For God's sake, he's gone insane! He's talking to his dead wife! He'll be the death of you! Let us go now, and Sergei won't kill you!"

They look back and forth from me to him.

A couple of them start edging for the door.

"If I tell Sergei to spare you, he will!" I'm pleading now. I look over at Darya. She isn't moving at all, and I can't tell if she's even breathing.

And then I hear shouts, and gunshots, and I lunge for the knife that's lying on the floor.

SERGEI

Icy wind whips my face as my men and I rush towards the old pulp mill. Dozens of us, clad in body armor, bristling with weapons.

It's an excellent bet that this is where Cataha and his men have taken Willow. It fits the description that Sabina gave us, down to the chemical smell.

And it's where Ludmilla's GPS tracker led us.

She was the one who sent us the email this morning. Or rather, she set it up for auto-delivery days ago.

Sergei, if you get this, it means that Cataha has betrayed me. I delivered Willow to Cataha so that he would return my sister to me. I used Darya as bait. In case Cataha double crosses me, I put a GPS tracker in my body and set up this email to be sent to you if I don't return home. Here are the coordinates. She listed a string of numbers. *I know I will burn in hell for this, but I had to do whatever I needed to do, to save my sister.*

I am praying that Willow is here. And that her father hasn't murdered her yet.

She is alive, she must be. I'd feel it if she were dead.

Ludmilla will be here too. That treacherous whore. If she's alive, she won't be for long.

Andrei leads the charge, blasting open the door that leads into the building.

As we make our way in, four men are rushing down the hall towards us, hands in the air, their faces wild with terror. "We surrender!" one of them screams. "Willow said if we helped you, you wouldn't kill us! We'll take you to her, we'll do it!"

What the hell is going on in there?

We keep our guns trained on them as we run down the hallway, turn right, down another hallway, and into a room that stinks of blood and acid and burning flesh.

Two women on tables. One dead, her throat gaping open – Ludmilla. Half of Darya's face is abraded and raw, the skin burned away.

Vasily's men are standing back, watching – *as Willow stabs Vasily in the gut.* Her face is battered and swollen, there's a filthy bandage taped to her nose, and I barely recognize her. Her hair is sticking up at crazy angles, the extensions gone.

As my men and I rush in, the guards don't even try to put up a fight. They all throw their arms up and sink to their knees.

Vasily's face is dumb with shock. The front of his shirt is dark with his blood.

Willow is screaming at him as she raises the knife again,

wordlessly, like a wild beast, her face twisted into a horrible mask, and I feel as if the knife is going into my own heart. Because this is my fault. I failed to keep her safe.

The knife plunges into his stomach one more time, and he howls in agony. I reach them, and Andrei pulls her off Vasily.

Then I unleash my full fury on her father, fists and boots. His screams rip the air apart and call to the savage beast inside me.

Bones are snapping. Blood sprays in hot, wet arcs.

This isn't my usual slow, deliberate kill. I've lost all control. Pyotr's shrill cries are in my ears again, and I am crushing and stamping like a madman. Slavik is by my side, stomping Vasily's leg so hard that bones protrude. Slavik was Vasily's victim too. His back still bears the scars of the men who got off on stubbing out their cigars on his flesh.

Vasily is gurgling out pleas for mercy. Mercy of the kind his family never showed to me.

Until all too soon he's silent. A pulped, bloody mess on the floor, a human shit-pile.

I glance up at Andrei. He's shielding Willow with his body as she sags against him, her eyes unfocused. Darya is gone – my men must have taken her from the room already.

I hurry over and gather Willow into my arms, lifting her like a child, and a million-ton weight lifts from my shoulders. She rests her battered face on my shoulder with a whimper that tears my heart.

As I leave, I flick a glance at Andrei. "Restrain the guards."

"She said you wouldn't kill us!" one of them screams in protest. I see six in this room, all on their knees. One of them reaches for his gun, and Andrei blows his head off before I can even blink.

I only hire the best.

"I won't kill you. We're turning you in to the police for kidnapping, assault and rape. Enjoy prison, bitches," I growl, and I hurry from the room. We have a helicopter waiting outside, and my Willow needs to be in the hospital.

CHAPTER TWENTY-THREE

Day seventeen...

Willow is finally resting at a hospital in St. Petersburg. I had her treated at a local hospital in Pevlovagrad, then flown here to this world-class hospital where she would receive the finest care.

Willow's got a broken nose, ribs, and a fractured fibula. Darya lost the sight in her right eye and needs extensive skin grafts on the right side of her face.

I sit by Willow's side every day. I read to her. I talk to her about our future. I tell her how the wedding preparations are going.

She's quieter than usual.

She's not at all bothered that she stabbed the man who used to be her father and watched him die. That, she's completely at peace with. It's the fact that she was forced to kill a helpless, restrained woman, even a woman as vile as Ludmilla, that has dampened her inner fire. I've told her again and again that Ludmilla would have died either way, that she saved Darya's life by doing what she did.

I don't know if it's penetrating through the fog of sadness that envelops her, because she's lost in a silent world I'm not a part of.

This hurts me. Seeing her suffer is a continuing rebuke to me, and makes me feel like I've failed on a level that I've never experienced before. The only thing in the world that I want is her happiness, and that is something that I can't obtain with money or threats or even kind, loving words, apparently. It's the first time I've ever wanted something I couldn't have.

I fly her family to my house in Sweden, in preparation for the wedding. As her body slowly heals, she talks to them every day via Skype.

Four days before our wedding, I make sure she's comfortable in her hospital bed, she has water by her bedside, she's eaten breakfast, and she wants for nothing. I make sure the private nurse that I hired to cater to her every wish is stationed in the room.

I leave to make some business phone calls, to deal with issues from suppliers and vendors and a million other issues that have piled up while I've concentrated on Willow and her slow, sad recovery.

When I return, she is gone. I feel as if I've been knocked off my feet.

There is a hand-written note on the night table. I read it, my heart sinking lower and lower with every word. "If you really love me, you will understand. It has to be my choice."

Day thirty...

It's April, a year from the time when I took Willow from

her uncle's home. The day is unseasonably mild for this time of year in Sweden. The clouds have parted, and sun beams down on us coldly.

And I am surrounded by a crowd on what should be my wedding day, but I am completely alone.

Slavik and Andrei are there, and Jasha, Anastasia, Yuri and Helenka. They're playing with Lukas while Kris and Marya watch. Darya is there as well. The right side of her face is still bandaged. Grigor is with her, hovering attentively. When she was first admitted to the hospital, while Willow was in surgery, I contacted him myself, because I knew it was what Willow would have done if she could. He dropped everything and flew to the hospital in St. Petersburg to be by her side.

Since the day Willow left, none of us have heard a word from her, but I insisted that we prepare anyway. Is she still in Russia? Has she returned to Sweden? I don't have a clue. I've got all my men looking for her, but this is a girl who knows how to live off the grid. I am sure that she has multiple fake identities and paperwork to back it up, so I won't know if she's crossed the border or not.

We're in a room that's been cleared of all furniture and decorated for my wedding day. The cake is a big white buttercream concoction. It's decorated with a man and a woman standing under a willow tree. I think she'd like that touch.

If only she were here.

I am a stubborn fool. I insisted on going forward with the wedding arrangements, and nobody dared to argue with me. It's a show of faith in our relationship, or a desperate plea, I'm not sure which.

Please come back to me, Willow. Please choose me.

There are white roses everywhere. An arch made of willow boughs over the doorway.

I am wearing a tuxedo. The priest is here, waiting.

I risk looking like a fool.

Stupid thoughts intrude.

Willow won't have time to change. It's 12:05 and we were supposed to get married at noon.

Who am I kidding? She's not coming. I know that. Why would I expect more? Why would I deserve more? She is beautiful, and kind, and too good for my world, the world I dragged her into without sparing a moment's thought for how much I was hurting her. The things I've done to her... she should run away. Far, far away.

But just because I deserve that doesn't mean I wanted her to.

Yuri walks up to me and pulls on my sleeve. "When is Willow getting here?" he demands.

"Shhh!" His sister elbows him. Because she doesn't think Willow is coming. She grabs him by the arm and marches him off, protesting.

The time has come, and now the minutes are ticking by. I won't leave the room today. Not until the sun goes down. The small crowd is milling around, avoiding my gaze, murmuring to each other.

I walk to the back of the room, where the bar is set up, and I have the bartender pour me a double shot of vodka. I down it one long, burning gulp.

The murmur of the crowd grows louder.

"Hey!" a breathless voice cries out from behind me, and my heart leaps into my throat.

Willow is running past everyone, limping on the leg that still has a cast on it, making her way towards me, gasping for breath. "Oh, my God, I am so sorry. Every single thing went wrong today. The plane was late. The cab ran into so much traffic. My cell phone died." She's near tears. My heart sings with joy. The heaviness that's been pressing me down into the earth falls away, and I am almost floating, I'm so light and free now.

It had to be her choice. And she chose me.

I grab her and pull her to me and smell her sweetness. Her warmth melts me, and I blink hard because my eyes are stinging.

Everyone is staring at us, and the mood has shifted. The room is full of sunshine now.

"Do you have the dress?" she asks me, still breathless. She's wearing jeans and sneakers. *And my engagement ring.*

"Never mind the dress. We're getting married right now."

"Right now? Like, this minute?" Her eyes widen as she looks up at me. "Don't you want to wait for me to put on some makeup or something?" Her face is clean and bare and beautiful. Her bruises are mostly faded. Her short, dark-blonde hair is messy and wavy, and I can't wait to sink my fingers into it.

I lean in. "You're already going to get the ass-whipping of a lifetime for pulling this little stunt. Believe me, it's going to be a wedding night to remember. For every minute that you make me wait, it adds to your punishment. Understand?"

"Yes, sir," she whispers, and there's a gleam of anticipation in her beautiful blue eyes.

"And Willow?"

"Yes, sir?" Her head is tipped back, her lips parted, and she's lucky that there's a room full of people and a priest looking at us right now, because otherwise she'd be bent over a table screaming for mercy.

My heart swells with love and gratitude and relief.

"I love you so much, sweetheart. Thank you for coming back to me. Thank you, a million times. I don't deserve it, but since you are doing me the honor of agreeing to be my wife, I vow to protect you and to dedicate my life to making you happy."

EPILOGUE

A year and a half later…
WILLOW

We live most of the year in Marslov now, but we've come back to the house in California to visit my family.

Sergei and I have taken Tatiana for a walk in the rose gardens, and he's cradling our daughter in his big arms as if she's a precious jewel. She's nine months old, fat-cheeked and happy. Two of her teeth just came in, so we're finally getting some sleep.

Lukas is so proud to be an uncle that he could just about burst. He's already drawn us so many beautiful pictures of her that we've bound them into a book. He's home in Sweden, because he's been enrolled in school, living a normal, settled life. Kris and Marya are his caretakers, but he knows the truth – that I'm his sister, and that I will always love him and be there for him. We'll bring him here next summer for vacation.

Tatiana is babbling when Sergei suddenly stops dead. He stares at our daughter's face in amazement.

"Did you hear that?" he cries out to me.

"Hear what?" I hurry over, worried. Is something wrong? Is she choking? Coughing?

Then I see that he's looking at her with so much love and pride that it's transformed his rough face into something almost angelic.

"Say it again," he croons at her. "Dada."

"Da. Da," she crows, and waves her fat pink fists.

"Oh my God," I cry out in wonder. "Talking already." I mock pout at him. "And she's a daddy's girl!" I lean in and give her my biggest smile. I stroke her fat cheek with my finger, and she gurgles with joy.

"Sweetie," I croon. "Who carried you in her belly for nine months? Who loves her baby? Me. Say 'Mama'. Mama, Mama."

She breaks into a huge smile, with her two little top teeth showing. She waves her chubby fist. *"Dada."*

Sergei throws back his head and roars with laughter, and I pretend to be angry with him, but truly, I'm glowing like the sun.

When I was growing up, I could never have dreamed of such happiness. Such freedom. Such love.

Darya and Grigor are coming to visit us next week. They married shortly after we did, and she's expecting.

The surgery has helped a lot. She'll never gain the vision back in her right eye, though. But Grigor tells her she's beautiful all the time.

She's still working at *Reforma*, and she loves it. Sergei bought Grigor his own auto repair shop in St. Petersburg, and business is thriving.

Sergei is the roof for Grigor's business, but he provides his services for free. Because it's still not possible to do business there without a roof. Some things will never change, unfortunately, but a lot has.

Nobody else has come into the Pevlova Oblast to replace *Cataha*. A few have tried, and every time, Sergei's people have wiped them out to the last man.

The police chief's family were able to come back home. There's a brand new Akim at *Reforma*, and the paper continues to thrive and grow. Sergei's construction, shipping and warehouse business are all entirely legit now, and he's opened up a new brick factory in Pevlovagrad to supply his construction company, and also invested in turning it into a tech center, creating jobs and hope there.

SERGEI

Later that evening, I have our nanny take Tatiana, and I take Willow by the hand and lead her into our bedroom. It's in a separate wing of the house, so I have her all to myself.

And it's soundproofed.

I shut the door behind me.

"You've been a bad girl," I tell Willow.

Her eyes widen with indignation. "I have not!" she protests. "What did I do?"

"Well, first of all, we're in our bedroom, and you forgot to say sir. We agreed."

"Did I ever agree to that?" she sniffs. "As I recall, on our honeymoon, *you* ordered me to say sir whenever we were in the bedroom, and I couldn't argue because I had a ball gag in my mouth."

A smile curves my lips.

I love it when she talks back to me. And I love that the dress she's wearing is so light and filmy.

"And secondly," I continue, "and a much graver offense. I hear that you've been working to undermine my authority with the troops." At her puzzled look, I explain. "Rumor has it that you spent all day long trying to get Tatiana to say Mama instead of Dada. There I was, slaving away in my office, talking to suppliers, securing our future, and you were betraying me. You even bribed her with sweets."

She gasps. She does not even try to deny her treachery. What would be the point? Her eyes are enormous, her mouth an O of shock. Her breathing quickens, betraying her arousal.

"How did you know?"

"How did you know, *sir?*" I correct her.

She starts to argue, then sees the look in my eyes. "How did you know, sir?"

"Sweetheart." I look at her mournfully as I shake my head. "Come on. That's almost insulting. I always know what you're doing, every minute of every day. Because you're mine, and I pay particularly close attention to the activities of my favorite piece of property. And you love that."

She narrows her eyes at me. "Only sometimes, *sir.* Other times it drives me crazy."

"How unfortunate for you. Because I'm never going to change, and you're never getting rid of me. Now, you've got two strikes against you, and you know what comes next."

I look down at her, at the dreamy look on her beautiful face.

"Yes, sir," she whispers, her gaze cast downward. Her nipples are hard. Which is perfect for what's coming next.

I point at the wooden box that I've place on the night-stand. "Walk over there and pick out your punishment."

She walks slowly, and when she opens the box, I see her look of confusion.

She reaches in and pulls out a silver pair of nipple

clamps, with little weights dangling from them. "That's all that's in the box."

"What a shame." I'm taking off my shirt while we speak. As I walk over to her, she backs up against the bed and stifles a cry.

"Those look as if they really hurt!" she protests.

"Yes, that's exactly the point. That's why it's called punishment."

"But...I'll be a really good girl. I'll go down on my knees. I'll suck your cock." She looks at me hopefully. I reach out and grab the front of her dress and rip it, and she jerks back with a curse.

"I loved that dress!"

She isn't wearing a bra, and her breasts are exposed to me now. The shreds of her dress slide off her shoulders and hang around her waist.

"Oh, boo hoo. I can buy you ten new ones. Put your hands behind your back. Now." That last part comes out on a vicious growl, and I am rewarded with her gasp of fear.

It doesn't matter that we're married, that she's the love of my life. It hasn't changed my essential nature. I am still a man who will be obeyed, and I can still deal out serious pain when she defies me.

She quickly puts her hands behind her back. I grab her left nipple and pull it towards me, and she grimaces in pain as I snap one of the nipple clamps onto the tender flesh.

I am rewarded with her sharp hiss of pain.

I lean in and suck her right nipple, that sweet little rosebud. Then I nip it hard enough to make her yelp in pain, and quickly snap the nipple clamp on. This time she can't keep from crying out.

"Sir! Please! Sir, it really hurts!" she wails. Tears are welling in her eyes, and I see her trembling from the effort it's taking her to keep her hands behind her back, to refrain from freeing her breasts from their torment.

She should know better by now. Her pleas have a direct effect on my cock. They make it really hard.

"On your knees, and those clamps don't come off until you've sucked me off and swallowed my come."

"You bastard," she hisses, but she sinks down as I'm freeing my cock from my slacks, and she takes me in her mouth faster than she ever has before, engulfing me in her wet heat.

Her head bobs, and she sucks and sucks, her tongue swirling. She strokes my balls with her fingers as she mouths my stiff member and one hand grasps the base.

"Yes," I groan. "That's it, sweetheart. So good."

I groan in pleasure as she begins moving up and down, tormenting and pleasing me with sensation.

Heat burns through my body, racing down my nerves. The pleasure grows and grows, and I'm about to come when I manage to pull myself back from the precipice. I grab her hair and pull her off me just in time. I almost exploded in her mouth, but I'm not ready yet.

Because I'm in control.

I'm always in control.

"Please!" she wails.

"On the bed. Hands and knees. Back right up to the edge."

"You promised!"

"I'm a lying motherfucker. Do it!" I bark at her.

She scrambles to obey.

When I slide my cock into her tight pussy, she's so wet that she's oozing.

"Mmmm." Her tortured moan of pleasure nearly makes me come right there. But I won't come alone.

I reach around and find her clitoris, pushing back the hood and rubbing the sensitive nub, pounding into her again and again. Every thrust makes the weights on the nipple clamps swing, and her wails are a mix of pain and pleasure. She slams back against me, urging me on.

I pause. "What's your name?"

She doesn't even hesitate. I've trained her too well.

"Willow Volkov!"

"And who's your master?"

"You are, sir! Please let me come, please, please, please!" She's forgotten about the pain of the nipple clamps, because the sweet agony of her desire is a far worse torture.

So I give my love what she wants. I pump into her again and again until she shudders and convulses, her tight sheath squeezing my cock. My own climax crashes down on me, hard, and I explode, filling her with my hot seed. No condoms anymore. I hope I'm putting another baby in her, another beautiful baby in my beautiful wife. I'd love to see her belly swell again, her breasts heavy with milk, her nipples darkening.

Then I slide the nipple clamps off her, and she slumps to the bed, moaning in relief. I lie down next to her and wrap my arms around her. Her back is to me, and she squirms in pleasure as I begin stroking her arm. She's so soft, so yielding. My cock is still half hard as I press it against her ass. I'll be ready for round two within minutes. And she'd better be ready to receive my cock anywhere I choose to put it.

"Willow Volkov," she sighs again, as if to remind herself, and she presses back against me and we melt together as if we're one.

Thank you so much for taking this journey with Willow and Sergei!

I'm very active on my Facebook page, at www.facebook.com/gingertalbot - come say hi!

For freebies, contests, and news of my latest releases, you can sign up to my newsletter at http://geni.us/Gingertalbot

THE END

Made in the USA
Coppell, TX
10 January 2020